STINK

WORST. FAIRY.
EVER.

First published in Great Britain in 2023 by Farshore
An imprint of HarperCollins*Publishers*
1 London Bridge Street, London SE1 9GF

farshore.co.uk

HarperCollins*Publishers*
Macken House, 39/40 Mayor Street Upper, Dublin 1, D01 C9W8, Ireland

Text and illustration copyright © Jenny McLachlan 2023

The moral rights of the author and illustrator have been asserted

ISBN 978 0 0085 2427 2

Printed and bound in the UK using 100% renewable electricity at
CPI Group (UK) Ltd

1

A CIP catalogue record for this title is available from the British Library.

Stay safe online. Any website addresses listed in this book are correct at the time of
going to print. However, Farshore is not responsible for content hosted by third
parties. Please be aware that online content can be subject to change and websites
can contain content that is unsuitable for children. We advise that all children are
supervised when using the internet.

MIX
Paper from
responsible sources
FSC™ C007454

This book is produced from independently certified FSC™ paper
to ensure responsible forest management.

For more information visit: www.harpercollins.co.uk/green

For Nick, Gemma,
Eric and Audrey

STINK

WORST. FAIRY. EVER.

WORDS AND PICTURES BY

JENNY McLACHLAN

Farshore

1. STRANGE TUESDAY

Something strange has happened to me.

It's so massively strange that I've decided to write this diary so I don't forget a single thing.

If this diary is ever turned into a film (which il probably will be) then the actor who plays me, Danny Todd, needs to be eleven, small (but strong), handsome, good at drawing, funny and look like this.

Right, back to the strange thing.

It began this morning when I went downstairs to open my birthday presents. I got six. Five were good and one was bad. I've put them in a list. I'll let you decide if the list goes from good to bad, or bad to good. P.S. I've kept one of the presents a mystery.

TWO RATS

CASH! £20

brush pens

ANT POWER HANDGRIPS

BIG ← CHOC

?→

danny xXx

I'm excited about the rats. I've wanted rats for ages and now I've got two. I've called them Tony and Noah because Mum will only let us have pets if we give them human names.

Cash is always good.

The brush pens are amazing because I draw cartoons about a fox called Mystic Ginger who wears a cloak.

Every one of my Mystic Ginger cartoons ends up with Mystic Ginger about to die in a terrible way.

Like this ...   Or this ...

What a lovely day for a swim, thought Ginger.

Trapped in cheese at a cheese party.

I got the hand grips so I can get muscly fists before I start secondary school. I actually wanted **DEADLY VIPER HAND GRIPS** like my best friend Kabir, but Dad says mine are better because ants have a better grip than vipers (plus, I looked on Amazon and they were ten pounds cheaper).

The massive bar of chocolate was from my mean-but-boring big-sister, Jasmine.

The mystery present was from my kind-but-wild little sister, Sophie. 'Got you this, Danny,' she said then she threw a badly wrapped present at my face. She can't help her wrapping or her throwing — she's only three — but Mum and Dad should have supervised her present buying.

Because when I ripped off the paper
I discovered Sophie had got me this.

That's right. A
fairy door. You're
supposed to stick
it to your bedroom
wall and it does . . .
absolutely nothing.
It just looks like
you've got a fairy
door stuck to your
bedroom wall.

'Oh great,' I said, sarcastically. 'Just what I've
always wanted . . . *NOT*.'

Mum told me off for being mean, but we all
knew Sophie had chosen a present for herself.

Before I could take the fairy door out of
its box and see if the little letter box opened,
Sophie snatched it out of my hands and ran
upstairs with it, cackling like a witch.

Mum, Dad and Jasmine thought this was

really funny, but I told them I was one present down now, and they owed me another one.

Mum said I was spoilt and to teach me a lesson she ate a row of my chocolate bar.

NOM

NOM

NOM

Then I said that I was TWO presents down so Dad and Jasmine both ate a row of my chocolate bar.

Big dad chomps

NIBBLE NIBBLE

I shut up after that.

I spent the rest of the day eating chocolate, training Tony and Noah and giving myself fists like Iron Man.

Then IT happened. The strange thing and the reason I'm writing this diary.

2. SOPHIE AND THE GLUE

I was using my new powerfully strong fists to carry Tony and Noah's cage into my bedroom when I discovered Sophie had been on a sticking spree with Superglue.

She had stuck:

A ball of stuff

3 Coco Pops

5 Cheerios

A cow

3 LEGO bricks

The fairy door

A piece of toast

A Disney prince

Not only had she stuck the fairy door to my bedroom wall she'd stuck a load of other stuff too and she'd done it really badly.

She hadn't even fled the scene of the crime. She was crouched down next to the fairy door and whispering into the tiny letter box, 'Hello, fairy . . . are you in there?'

I was so angry I did something mean.

Soph, you're doing it all wrong.

Why?

Because every fairy door has a real fairy behind it, waiting to come out, but you have to do something special to set it free.

I don't believe you, Danny. You're tricking me.

I PROMISE you, Sophie. There is a lovely fairy behind that door. She's gorgeous and she smells of sweets and I'm going to get her to come out and meet you.

Thank you, Danny!

THANK YOU!

THANK YOU!

THANK YOU!

Do it now!

PLEEEASE!

I know, it was a rubbish rhyme, but I was making it up on the spot.

Sophie got so excited that she made her hands go like a starfish and she started panting like our dog, Frida. She looked so funny that I started laughing.

And that's when the fairy door exploded off the wall and hit me in the face.

I fell to the ground clutching my nose and when I opened my eyes I saw this . . .

That's right. A real live fairy had come out of the fairy door and was standing in my bedroom surrounded by smoke and stars, and she looked nothing like the fairy on the box.

Suddenly the smoke and stars were sucked through the hole in the wall. Then the fairy picked up the door and used her wand to screw it back into place. Then she turned and ran towards me and half-flew, half-scrabbled up my body until she was fluttering in front of my face.

'I belong to YOU, Boy,' she said, poking me in the forehead with her wand. 'You are my master and I will stay by your side until you DIE!'

'But, but, but . . . I don't want you!' I shouted.

'Not true. You said I was gorgeous and smelled of sweets!'

'I was being sarcastic!' I whimpered.

'Tough,' she said. 'If you didn't want me you shouldn't have called me out of Fairyland using the ancient humany-fairy-sacred-ritual and done all those magic words, should you?'

'But I made them all up!' I said, and then I started to cry because for some reason the fairy had decided to jab her wand into my nose again and again.

For the record, Sophie wasn't looking scared or crying. No, she was gazing al lhe fairy with a look of total love on her face.

At this point I decided to do what I always do when I'm scared or need something.

MUM!

Quick as a flash, the fairy whipped out her wand and shouted,

RED!

Stars exploded, I tasted strawberry laces and then my lips glued together.

Next the fairy zoomed close to my eyes and hissed, 'Do anything else, Boy, and I'll BITE you!'

So I ran towards the door and she bit me.

My ear bits

3. The Biting

During all this Sophie did nothing _AT ALL_ to help me. She just sat there with her mouth hanging open like she does when she watches _Timmy Time._

If Sophie had wanted to help me she could have squashed that fairy in one of her sticky fists.

The fairy nibbled my ear like it was a corn on the cob. Luckily for me she's got a small mouth and even smaller teeth.

My ear

Then she flew back in front of my
face and hissed, 'Right, Boy, listen to me.
There's something you need to know about
fairies. If a grown-up ever sees us we DIE.
Do you understand?'

I nodded and went 'Mmmgmmpff'
(because my lips were still stuck together).

'And we don't die nicely by disappearing
in a puff of pink glittery smoke.
Oh no. We MELT!'

'Noooooooo!' wailed Sophie.

The fairy hadn't finished. 'And when we melt
we turn into magic goo that can burn holes
through ANYTHING. Do you want that to happen,

Boy? Do you want to be a fairy killer who burns holes through their house with magic goo?'

I shook my head.

The fairy smiled and said, 'Good! Now if I undo the spell do you promise to keep quiet?'

Nod nod (I went).

She tapped my lips with her wand, said, 'DER' and my lips unglued.

DER!

Then she grinned, all pleased with herself. 'Did you see what I did there? I said RED backwards – DER – and that undid the spell. That's the first time it's ever worked!'

Next me and the fairy had a serious conversation. It was like a business meeting and it went like this . . .

So you want me to go away?

Yes please! I don't want a fairy. I'm starting secondary school soon and I can't take you with me.

Secondly school? What's that? I want to see it!

No you really don't. You need to go back through the fairy door and leave me alone.

Well there is ONE thing you can do to make me go away.

What? Tell me! I'll do anything!

Give me cash.

'I can do that,' I said. 'Nan's given me twenty pounds for my birthday.'

But the fairy said, 'I don't want your rubbish old Nan pounds. I want fairy nuggets.'

Then she gave me a lecture on nuggets. She has insisted on writing this bit and helping me draw the pictures.

Nuggets is fairy money. I've heard about your stinky old human pounds and stuff and it sounds rubbish, but nuggets are great because they can buy you anything. I've got three nuggets in my troll bank and that's not even enough to pay my rent which is five nuggets a week. That's why I got a job with F.A.R.T. Don't laugh, Boy. F.A.R.T. isn't funny at all.

I said, DON'T LAUGH! F.A.R.T. stands for Fairy Assistance Response Team.

F.A.R.T.

ALES AUXILIUM

For every good deed I do to help a human I earn ONE HUNDRED nuggets and I really, really need them because my wings are basically all busted up and I need new ones. The best ones are Silver Bullets – that's what my brother Fandango has got.

He's got tons of nuggets. He's got so many nuggets he's got a wig made of mermaid hairs and a pet gnome called Ellis. I hate him. Fandango not Ellis. Actually I hate Ellis too.

Anyway, if I help a human being by doing a good deed and get my one hundred nuggets then I promise that I will go away FOR EVER.

So I said, 'Really? You promise to go away as soon as you get one hundred nuggets?'

At this point the fairy flew back in front of my face. It took a lot of effort because her wings really are rubbish. Her cheeks puffed out and she batted her wings like mad.

Then she said, 'I PROMISE, Boy, and one thing you should know is that . . .'

FAIRIES NEVER LIE!

4. Getting to know my fairy

At this point Dad took Sophie to bed.

'Noooooo! Noooooo!' she screamed putting her hands in Dad's mouth and trying to pull his face apart. 'I want to stay with Danny and his fairy!'

Dad laughed as Sophie tried to break his nose and then his specs. 'Oh no you don't, young lady. No more playing with Danny and his fairy for you. It's bed-time!'

'He's got a FAIRY in his HAIR!' she yelled as Dad carried her out of the room.

It was true. I did have a fairy in my hair.

You see, the second Dad came into my bedroom the fairy shot inside my hair and stayed there.

I could feel her trembling all the time Dad was in the room so she must have been telling the truth about the whole magic goo thing. I was trembling too. I really didn't want magic goo burning through my skull and into my brain.

Anyway, after Dad and Sophie left I shook the fairy out of my hair and on to my bed.

Then she explored my bedroom.

Clearly she loved the rats.

'WOW!' she said when she saw them. 'Baby dragons!'

'No, they're rats,' I said, but she wasn't having any of it.

'I know a baby dragon when I see one, Boy. My brother Fandango would be so jealous if he saw me riding around Fairyland on one of these!'

'Look,' I said. 'If I really am your master then you should know my name. It's Danny Todd.'

'HA!' said the fairy. 'Todd means "armpit" in Fairyland!'

'No it doesn't,' I said.

'Yes it does. You're basically called Danny Armpit.'

'Whatever,' I said, deciding to be mature about this.

Danny
Todd's
todd

Then I held out my hand and said, 'It's nice to meet you.'

The fairy shook my middle finger between her two tiny hands.

'Nice to meet you too, Danny Todd. My name is S dot Tink.'

'S dot Tink?' I said, not sure if I'd heard right.

'Are you stupid or something, Danny?' she said, then she flew over to my LEGO and arranged the bricks so they looked like this:

'So you're called Stink?' I said.

This enraged her. She growled and hissed and showed her teeth. Then she threw the piece of LEGO that was supposed to be a full stop at me.

'No, you IDIOT! My name is *S dot Tink*. Tink is my surname — it's a very common surname in Fairyland — and "S" is how my first name *starts*.'

'So what is your first name?'

Stink's eyes bulged and she clutched her heart. 'Danny, never EVER ask a fairy what their name is. It's really rude. It's like showing someone your bum. Would you show someone your bum, Danny? No. So never ask what my name is EVER AGAIN.'

(I once did show someone my bum, two people actually, but it was an accident. Mum noticed that new people were moving in to our road and invited their children (Poppy and Fin Budgen) round to play. What she didn't know was that me and Jasmine had set up a waterslide and I'd discovered that swimming trunks ruined my glide. So this is how Poppy and Fin met me.)

But S dot Tink

takes too long to say so I'm calling her Stink.

And that's it. The end of my *strange day*.

Right now Stink is curled up between
my rats because she's
decided that's where
she's going to sleep.

She's taken over
their cage. Their plastic

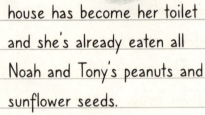

house has become her toilet
and she's already eaten all
Noah and Tony's peanuts and
sunflower seeds.

I'm going to bed now.
I need all the energy I can
get because tomorrow I'm
going to help Stink do her
good deed. Fingers crossed,
by tomorrow evening she'll
be gone!

5. Wednesday

She's not gone. She's riding round my bedroom on Noah, eating a woodlouse and wearing one of my socks.

She hasn't done a single good deed today. If anything, all she's done are bad deeds.

It started to go wrong at breakfast.

I was eating Cheerios and Stink was sitting on the edge of my bowl, occasionally fishing a Cheerio out with her wand.

'How does this good deed thing work?' I asked.

'I help humans and then my boss at F.A.R.T., Melville, decides if I deserve one hundred nuggets.'

'How will you know when you've got your nuggets and can go back to Fairyland?' I asked.

She fluttered her tatty wings. 'Because these will change. I've already ordered a pair of Silver Bullets so if Melville puts the nuggets in my troll bank, BANG! New wings for S dot Tink!'

And no more fairy for Danny! I thought as I scooped up a spoonful of cereal.

Then Mum walked into the kitchen and

SWOOSH!

this happened.

6. Good Deeds

Stink's boiler suit was soaking so she took it off in my room then hung it on the radiator to dry.

Have you ever wondered what fairies wear under their boilersuits? This.

Then she bit holes in one of my socks and made it into a giant hoody.

'Let's go out,' she said, pressing her face against the window.

But there was no way I was letting her loose in the world. Instead I forced her to stay inside with me all day and do good deeds. Here's what we did:

Made Sophie a jam sandwich

Hung out the washing

Brushed Sophie's teeth

I've discovered that I can't leave Stink alone with Sophie for a second. They're a bad influence on each other. Here's a conversation I overheard:

Stink: Sophie, what do you want to do?

Sophie: Throw Danny's pens out of the window.

Stink: That, Sophie, is a brilliant idea. Let's throw some other things out too.

Sophie: Like what, Stink fairy?

Stink: Um . . . How about his clothes and stuff?

Sophie: And his PANTS.

Stink: Yes! Yes! Let's throw all his pants out of the window!

After I'd collected all my belongings from the garden, I asked Stink how throwing my pants out of the window could ever be considered a good deed.

'I don't have to do a good deed *for you*, Danny,' she said, like I was a massive fool. 'I have to do a good deed for a *human*. You're just the way I find out about the good deeds and the person who carries me around and stuff.'

So I'm Stink's good-deed taxi service.

I asked her what sort of things her fairy friends had done to earn one hundred nuggets.

'I've not got many friends,' she said (no surprise there), 'but Fandango used to work for F.A.R.T. and he's stinking rich so he must have done some massive good deeds.'

After a big think, Stink came up with this list of All the Best Stuff Fandango's Ever Done for F.A.R.T. In case you're wondering, Stink told me what to put in the pictures.

1. Folded 1000 origami cranes to make a Get Well Soon mobile for Kiko, the Crown Princess of Japan.

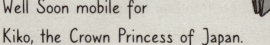

2. Used his tiny fairy body to plug a hole in a paddling pool and save four-year-old Minty Smith's birthday party.

3. Freed a cat with its head stuck in a bagel. (This was an extra good deed that he did on the way home from finding a dog who had been missing for three years.)

4. Enchanted a flock of starlings and made them spell out JOE to cheer up a sad bird watcher.

I asked Stink if she could enchant things. She said to learn awesome magic like that you had to go to 'university and sluff' and she couldn't be bothered. Apparently all she can do is make bees and ants fall asleep.

All in all it's been a hopeless day of Good Deeding, but Stink did do an OK job of entertaining Sophie in the bath. She did disguises using bubbles. Can you guess what they are?

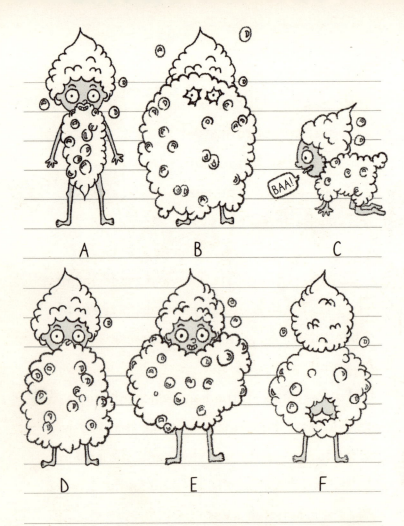

And now, like I said, she's riding round the room on Noah and eating a woodlouse.

A: A gnome. B: A cloud. C: A sheep.
D: Fog. E: Mist. F: A bum in mist

7. Still Wednesday

When Mum came into my room to say goodnight she told me something interesting. Apparently our miserable next-door neighbour, Professor Najin, has got a problem. Her garden is so overgrown it's become infested with foxes.

'It's all over the road WhatsApp group,' Mum said. 'The foxes are terrorising the neighbourhood like delinquents.'

'What are they doing?' I asked. 'Smashing windows and drinking beer?'

'Don't be silly, Danny,' said Mum. 'They've been pooing on crisp packets and knocking over bins.'

Then she grabbed my hand and said, 'Jasper Budgen from number ten has complained to the council and they're sending a pest controller round to poison them. Poisoning foxes, Danny!' She squeezed my hand hard. 'Can you imagine anything so barbaric?'

You should know that Mum and I disagree about almost everything. But one thing we DO agree on is foxes.

I love them so much that I've drawn 135 Mystic Ginger cartoons. Mum loves them so much she's got a fox tattooed on her arm. I love them so much that I pretend to like Leicester City Football Club just so I can get stuff with foxes on it. Mum loves them so much she has a stone fox on our doorstep that she dresses up in clothes. You get the idea.

We  foxes.

'There must be something we can do to stop them,' I said.

The idea came to me in a flash: a way to solve my fairy problem _and_ Professor Najin's fox problem all in one go.

'If I tidy up Professor Najin's garden then the foxes won't like it and they will go and live somewhere else!' These genius words burst out of me just like that.

Now, during this whole fox chat, Stink had been hiding behind my curtain. As soon as I mentioned tidying Najin's garden, she jumped out from behind the curtain and shook her head wildly. Then she did a double thumbs down.

Waft
Waft

Then she mimed doing a fart, held her nose and wafted her hand around in front of her face as if to say, 'Your idea stinks.'

Mum couldn't see any of this because her back was to the window.

I understood what Stink was saying. She didn't want to tidy up Professor Najin's garden and I knew why. She'd spent ages staring out of the window and knew how untidy it was.

But I've decided. It doesn't matter how many fart mimes Stink does, she's going to help me clear out the garden. Not only is it a nice thing to do for Professor Najin, who is old, it's also good for the foxes and the council because they won't have to waste money paying pest controllers.

Tomorrow Stink will be earning her one hundred nuggets and going back to Fairyland and I cannot wait!

The second Mum left the room, Stink flew up to my face, grabbed hold of my hair and dangled in front of my eyes.

'We are NOT going to tidy up that stupid garden, Danny Todd!'

'Oh yes we are,' I said. 'We're going to tidy up that garden better than anyone has EVER tidied up a garden before and you are going to get your wings and GO!'

8. Thursday

Luckily for me it's the summer holidays so this morning, straight after breakfast, I went round to Professor Najin's and rang on her doorbell.

I was wearing old clothes and carrying a spade and a pair of rusty secateurs. I had a fairy in my hair and a pair of gardening gloves on my hands. I was ready for GOOD DEED ACTION.

'Urrgh,' said Professor Najin when she opened the door and saw me standing there. 'It's you, the boy from next door. What do you want?'

You know what old ladies are supposed to be like? Well Professor Najin is the opposite of this.

Rumour has it Professor Najin used to be a swimming teacher and I can believe this because she always wears a whistle round her neck and she swims in the sea every day of the year. She's also good at giving orders and has a voice that would carry in a noisy swimming pool. Nobody knows what she's a professor in. It's a mystery.

'Hi,' I said. 'Please can I tidy your garden for you?'

Najin gave me one of her best stares. It chilled me to the core.

It made me feel so uncomfortable that cereal rose up my throat and I tasted milk and I even felt a bit of a Cheerio.

'Why would you EVER want to do that?' she said. 'I'm not giving you any money.'

Suddenly Stink's voice hissed in my ear, 'Let's go, Danny. This is a bad idea. I want to watch *Timmy Time* with Sophie.'

Ignoring her I said to Najin, 'I don't want money. I thought it would be a nice thing to do.'

Najin narrowed her eyes suspiciously and I knew why. She's known me all my life and I have never, ever tried to do a single nice thing for her.

'I don't believe you,' she said.

Quickly I told her that Jasper Budgen had complained to the council and that they were sending round a pest controller. Then I told her about my plan to get the foxes to move on.

'That's why I want to tidy your garden,'
I said. 'I'm doing it for the foxes. You see,
I love foxes.'
STARE goes Najin.
STARE STARE.
 STARE STARE STARE.
'So do I,' she said. 'Let yourself
in through the gate. You're not
allowed to use my toilet.'

BANG! She slammed the door in my face then
a second later her eyes appeared at the letter box.

'And make sure you clear up any mess you
make. And don't kill anything, not even a worm!'
Flap.
She was gone.

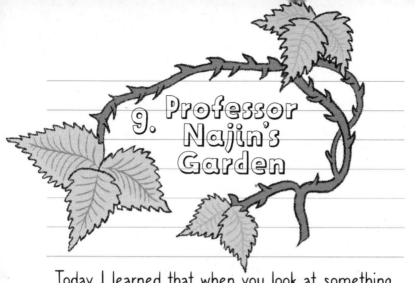

9. Professor Najin's Garden

Today I learned that when you look at something from a distance, like from a bedroom window, it looks better than it is in reality.

'What have you done, you IDIOT!' Stink said supportively. She was still in my hair but had stuck her head out to take a look around. 'This isn't a garden. It's a big fat mess. It's a disaster. It's an explosion of leaves! Look, that tree has grown a shed! There's a pond of fruit! And there are horses everywhere!'

'Those aren't horses,' I said. 'They're foxes.'

'Shows what you know, Danny. I had to read *Humanyland for Beginners* to get into F.A.R.T. and those things are *horses*.'

Either Stink didn't read *Humanyland for Beginners* very carefully or it's full of mistakes, because the creatures sunbathing in Najin's garden were 100% foxes.

I'd seen foxes slinking in and out of her place, but I didn't realise how many there were or how bold they'd become.

I pushed my way into the middle of the garden to the pond of fruit (a dried-up pond with a blackberry bush growing out of the middle of it) and looked around.

Stink was right about one thing. The garden was a mess. It was so bad that I wasn't sure where to begin so I put Stink on an empty bird bath and asked her what we should do first.

'How should I know?' she said, with a yawn.

'Because you work for F.A.R.T. and you're trained to assist humans,' I said, 'and I am a human and I need your assistance.'

She shrugged. 'To be honest, Danny, I wasn't listening during the training sessions.'

'If you don't at least TRY to help then you'll never get your Silver Bullet wings!' I said.

With a sigh, Stink got to her feet and said, 'Fine. I'll do some awesome magic.' Then she jumped off the edge of the bird bath and half-flew, half-fell to the ground.

Stink was completely hidden in the long grass so I used the secateurs to clear an arena for her to work in.

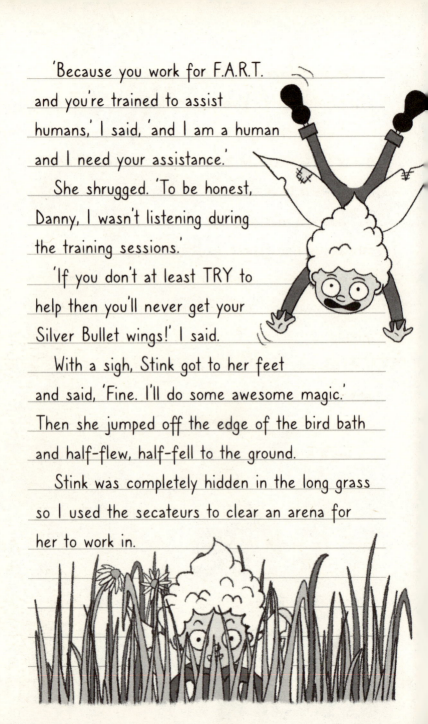

Next, she strode around the patch of grass psyching herself up. She punched her tiny fist into her other tiny fist and shouted, 'C'maaaan, S dot Tink, you can do this! You can teach this garden a lesson. You can DESTROY the green!'

Then she did a series of stretching exercises.

Finally, she strode into the middle of the clearing and got into position.

'You'd better get back, Danny,' she said. 'This is potent magic I'm about to unleash.'

I stood behind the bird bath.

'Further,' she said.

I stood behind the fox's deck chair.

'Further,' she said.

Further!

I stood behind the shed.

'That should be OK,' she said, or rather, screamed because by now I was standing a long way away.

Next she whipped out her wand and cried, 'GREEN SEVENTEEN!'

A shower of stars and blue smoke shot from the end of her wand and a bolt of light sliced through the sky towards the overgrown lawn. It was impressive!

Until the smoke cleared.

I couldn't believe it.

'Stink, do you know any spells that can do more damage than lethally destroying one blade of grass at a time?'

'Ha ha ha!' she went. 'I'm not a WARLOCK, Danny!' Then I heard a snigger . . .

STINK'S SPELLS

Apparently fairy spells are long and complicated so Stink has made shortcuts by giving them names of colours. She can undo a spell by saying the colour backwards. Here are all the spells I've seen her do so far:

Red – sticks things together, like my lips.

Green Seventeen – a blast capable of cutting one blade of grass in half.

Off White – Randomly changes the colour of things.

10.
The Terrible
Twins

The snigger was joined by another snigger. Then a sneery voice said all sneerily, 'What are you doing, Danny Todd?'

I looked up and saw this:

I know. Terrifying.

Stink took one look at the Budgen twins then flew into the air and dive-bombed into my hair.

'Are they grown-ups?' she whispered. I did a small shake of my head. 'Well, they've got big voices like grown-ups!'

Najin has two sets of next-door neighbours. The Todds on one side (us, the nice lot), and the Budgens on the other side (the nasty lot). Fin and Poppy go to my school and they are as mean, moany and show-offy as their mum and dad.

'Oi!' shouted Poppy. 'I said: what are you doing, Danny Todd?'

'Nothing,' I said.

Yes you were. We heard you doing a little squeaky voice.

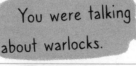

You were talking about warlocks.

You were playing a game!

And talking to yourself!

Then they laughed at exactly the same time like two evil robots.

Stink hissed in my ear, 'Make those two crumpet elves go away or I'm going to explode them like I exploded the grass!'

I was fairly certain that Stink's magic wasn't powerful enough to explode Poppy and Fin, but I didn't want to take the risk, so I said something that was certain to get rid of them.

'Yes, I was playing a game. Do you want to play with me?'

Poppy and Fin never want to have anything to do with me because I wear the wrong trainers, Dad puts whole boiled eggs in my lunch box, I'm rubbish at football and once, as mentioned earlier, I accidentally showed them my bum and this has made me a loser for life in their eyes.

SWIMMING TRUNKS RUIN THE GLIDE - EVERYONE KNOWS THAT!

No, we do not want to play with you. But we've got a message for you from my dad. He's getting our garden ready for my chocolate-themed birthday party on Saturday and he doesn't want any leaves or bits of grass coming over from Najin's side. He says, whatever you're doing out here, don't let ANYTHING come into our garden!

Yeah!

Then they disappeared behind the fence.

'YUCK!' yelled Stink, bursting out of my hair and flying around my face. 'You should have let me explode them!'

'Stick to the grass,' I said, then we got on with doing our excellent Good Deed.

11. Fox Fun

By the end of our first proper Doing a Good Deed Session, all Stink and I had managed to do was clear a small area of grass and Stink had almost certainly earned zero nuggets.

I know this because it was me who cut the grass with my secateurs. Stink knocked down seven blades with her Green Seventeen spell then said the magic had worn her out and spent the rest of the afternoon trying to ride a fox.

Stink has taken a shine to the fat fox and called it Rosie (even though she says it ran over her head when she was lying in the grass and it's *definitely* a boy).

There were a couple of moments when I thought Stink might get eaten by Rosie, but she managed to tame all the foxes using a spell called Off White*. Basically it changes the colour of things and it's the best spell I've seen Stink do.

Anyway, now Najin has the usual ginger foxes in her garden, plus a pink one, a black-and-white stripy one (Rosie), a yellow spotted one (the fox with half a tail) and a rainbow one (the smallest cub).

Professor Najin only came outside once during the whole day.

*see page 53

After lunch, she chucked a bowl of scraps into an enormous contraption by the back door.

Then she put her hands on it and said, 'This is my wormery. Don't touch!' and went back indoors.

I didn't get any warm biscuits straight out of the oven or glasses of too-strong orange squash. She didn't say to me, 'Here's a five-pound note for slaving away in my garden, Danny.'

Nope. All day Professor Najin just lay on her sofa watching old videos of the Olympics and eating crisps.

I know this because when I stood on the edge of the bird bath I could see through her French windows.

Videos. Who watches videos?? Professor Najin, that's who.

12. Rat Theft

After dinner, aching from a day spent hacking at grass, I walked into my bedroom and got a big shock.

That's right, Stink was trying to steal Noah and take him to Fairyland.

'Can't I borrow him for an hour?' she begged. 'Pleeeease, Danny. Fandango will be so jealous. He's always been better than me at everything and has way cooler stuff. If he saw me

riding around on a baby dragon it would be
the best thing EVER because it would make
him so sad.'

'NO!' I said, holding Noah protectively.

Then Stink did one of her most cunning looks.
The reason I know this cunning look
so well is because I've drawn it loads
of times in my Mystic
Ginger cartoons when
Ginger is about to do something
wicked.

'Danny,' she said. 'You know you said I had to
do my good deed and get my wings and go away?'

'Yes?'

'Why do you want me to go away so badly?'

I thought about lying, but Stink has a way of looking at me without blinking which makes it impossible to lie.

'Because that's when I start secondary school,' I said. 'I'm on holiday now, but I've got to go to school on Monday and then I won't be able to look after you.'

And in my head I thought: and there is no way EVER that I am starting secondary school with a fairy in my hair. The odds are already stacked against me. Mum made me get a blazer that's two sizes too big and she's making me wear a pair of Dad's work shoes that he says are too pointy and shiny to be seen in and Mum won't buy me a new rucksack even though mine has a unicorn on it. I didn't realise the unicorn

was there when I chose it.
I thought it was space. It is
space, only it's space arranged
into the shape of a unicorn.
I've used badges to try and hide the
unicorn, but it's got a massive horn and I don't
have enough badges to fully disguise it. Anyway,
the point is, I'm never EVER taking Stink to
secondary school.

Of course, I kept all this in my head, but it
was like Stink had heard every word.

You *really* want to get rid of
me, don't you, Danny Todd?

'No,' I lied. 'I just want you to have
new wings, that's all.'

'I tell you what. If you let me borrow Noah,
just for an hour or two, then I promise I'll pick
something up from my treehole that will clear
that garden in an hour, tops.'

'What's a treehole?'

'It's where I live. It's a hole. In a tree.'

I held Noah in my hands and he gently
sniffed my fingers. He gazed at me with his
beautiful black eyes then cleaned his whiskers
and gave me a couple of licks too.

'OK, you can have him for an hour,' I said.

Don't judge me. Remember my unicorn
rucksack and Dad's shoes.

We got Noah to go through the
fairy door by rolling a peanut in
there. He trotted after it and
Stink followed, yelling, 'BYE,
DANNY TODD!'

The door slammed shut
behind them.

I waited a few seconds then tried
the door. I wanted to see what Fairyland looked
like. The door was stuck fast. I guess only Stink
can open it. I had to make do with opening the
tiny letter box with a pen and peering inside.

I couldn't see much, but I got a whiff of that bad smell again — wet dog, old sandwiches, and a trace of something else . . . wrinkly mushrooms? Damp socks? — I really thought Fairyland would smell nicer.

So now Stink and Noah are gone and it's just me and Tony.

See. Here are Tony's lonely footprints.

I am worried about Noah, but mainly I can't stop thinking about what Stink is going to pick up from her treehole . . . A more powerful wand? Some sort of fairy weed killer? Fairy dust that turns grass into rainbows?

I can't wait to find out!

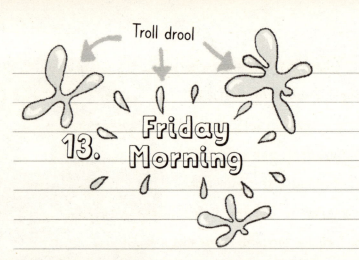

Troll drool

13. Friday Morning

It's a troll. Stink brought him back during the night and put him in Tony and Noah's cage. They're not happy about it.

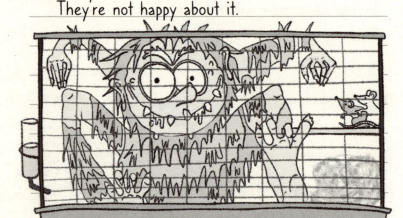

The first thing I asked Stink was how she got him through the fairy door because this troll is the size of Rosie the fat male fox.

'Oh, I used Yellow,' she said. 'It's a shrinking spell.'

I asked her why she hadn't used Yellow on Najin's long grass and she explained that the spell doesn't last for long. In fact, she only just managed to get the troll into the rats' cage before he grew back to his normal size.

'So you live with this troll in your treehole?' I said.

'No, he's my neighbour. He's got his own treehole,' she said. 'He eats my rubbish. That's why I've brought him here. Just think how quickly he's going to eat the stuff in Najin's garden!'

The troll yawned and I saw a mouthful of vicious-looking yellow teeth. They did look sharp . . .

Obviously having a troll in my bedroom is making me nervous, especially as Stink says they eat 'anything'. I've had to temporarily store Noah and Tony in my LEGO box.

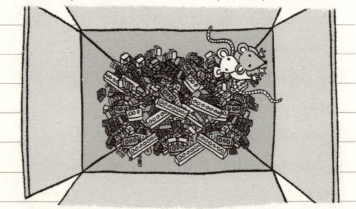

The troll is snuffling and growling in the rats' cage and I feel sick with worry. This whole fairy situation has got completely out of control.

I could tell Mum and Dad, but they'd insist on seeing Stink and then she'd melt and I'd be a fairy murderer AND stuck with a troll who's too big to go back to Fairyland.

I never thought being eleven would be this complicated.

The second Stink's got her new wings and gone back to Fairyland I am destroying that stupid fairy door.

14. Breakfast News Flash

Update. I just had a massive shock. Sophie came into the kitchen with her dolls' pram and there was something wriggling around in there. It was the troll! Sophie had put it in a babygro and tied it up with her tights. Straight away, Frida started sniffing around the pram.

Three things stopped my family from seeing the troll.

'Look! I found a monster in Danny's bedroom!' said Sophie.

'A monster . . . cool,' said Mum, turning a page.

'That's nice, Soph,' said Dad, sniffing his mug.

'*Shhhh!*' said Jasmine.

Stink was, as usual, hidden in my hair. 'Remember Trolls eat ANYTHING Danny!' she hissed in my ear.

Just then Sophie stuck her finger in the troll's mouth, saying, 'Nice monster!'

BARK!

BARK!

BARK!

BARK!

Frida went berserk, snarling and growling at the troll.

I had to act fast before Mum or Dad looked up. I decided to say the one thing I always try to avoid saying. 'Do you want me to play with you, Soph?'

Well this made Mum look up from her book faster than lightning. She narrowed her eyes suspiciously. 'I thought you were sorting out Professor Najin's garden, Danny. You're not trying to get out of it, are you?'

I had to get her eyes back on her book because of what was taking place behind her.

'Definitely not. I'll take Sophie with me. She can help!'

'OK,' said Mum happily. *Wspaniale! Teraz mogę się dowiedzieć, kto zabił mleczarza.**

Who lets their precious three-year-old daughter play in a garden full of foxes with an eleven-year-old babysitter? My mum when she's only got a few chapters left of her gruesome murder mystery, that's who.

So I dragged Sophie upstairs and told her to put on some old clothes while I wrote this. Fingers crossed, by the time I'm writing in you again, dear diary, I'll have good news for you!

(*Did I mention that Mum's Polish? She just said, 'Great! Now I can find out who killed the ferret.' Although I might have got some of that wrong.)

15. Friday Evening

I've only got bad news, I'm afraid. Stink is having a bath with Sophie and a troll is loose in our town.

Here's what happened.

Najin was a bit more friendly when I turned up with Sophie. She managed a flicker of a smile when she saw Sophie pushing her pram then said, 'You're still not allowed to use the toilet,' and went back to her videos. Today I noticed that she watched *Pirates of the Caribbean* as well as sailing races.

This might explain why Najin always wears flipflops and has bare legs. Perhaps she's a sailor. Do sailors use whistles?

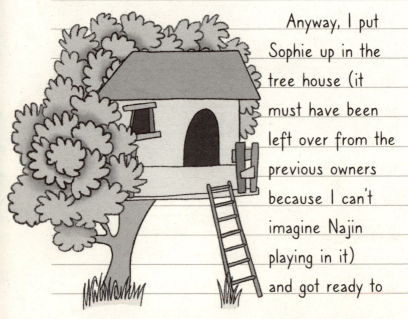

Anyway, I put Sophie up in the tree house (it must have been left over from the previous owners because I can't imagine Najin playing in it) and got ready to

release the troll so it could eat all the weeds.
For a girl who can't do up her own trousers
Sophie had tied that troll up good.

'Better let me take over,' said Stink. 'I think
it's angry.'

It did seem angry. In
fact, I started having
second thoughts
about letting it go.

'Are you sure
this is a good idea,
Stink?'

'It's an amazing
idea, Danny. We let
the troll eat all the
grass and weeds in
the garden – half
an hour should do it
– then I shrink it again
using the Yellow spell and
we shove it back into Fairyland.'

Put like this, it did sound like quite a good idea, but just to be on the safe side I climbed into the tree house and I sat next to Sophie. Then we got ready to see the troll do its work. The foxes were watching too from the safety of the shed roof.

'Here we go!' Stink shouted, then she undid the last knot in Sophie's tights.

The troll flew round the garden like a hungry tornado gobbling everything in its path.

To begin with it was brilliant. Soph and me were clapping and cheering and Stink was down on her bird table shouting out stuff like:

Eat the tree!

Eat the bush!

That's it! Eat the wheelbarrow too!

No. Don't eat the fox. Spit it out. SPIT IT OUT!

Here's what the troll ate:

17 bushes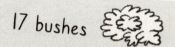

All the grass

6 trees

All the brambles

1 wheelbarrow

Loads of nettles

1 trolley

My best friend, Kabir

THE KID

K-BOB

iceman

16.
Kabir

SHREDZZZ

Maxximum

That's right. The troll ate the top half of my best friend Kabir.

I wasn't expecting Kabir to turn up. He must have called in at my house and been sent round by Mum. Poor Kabir, or rather, poor The Kid*.

He wandered into the back garden, saw me up in the tree house, said, 'Hi Danny. Hi Sophie,' then got swallowed, headfirst.

*Kabir's Nickname Failures

Ever since I met Kabir in Miss Shepherd's class in Year 1 he's been trying to get himself a nickname.

Here are his failed nicknames:
- K-Bob
- Maxximum (this one kind of stuck because sometimes he acts like a mum e.g. he keeps plasters and a pound in his pocket 'just in case' and he doesn't like getting muddy)
- Shredder or Shredzzz
- Iceman
- The Kid

I jumped down from the tree house and grabbed hold of Kabir's feet. Stink whipped out her wand ready to do a spell. Sophie laughed like it was the funniest thing she'd ever seen in her life.

It was Kabir's skateboard that saved his life. He carries this skateboard with him everywhere he goes (even though he can't skate) and one of the wheels got caught in the troll's teeth.

The troll coughed, I pulled and Kabir shot out of the troll's mouth along with a load of troll spit.

Straight away Stink yelled 'Yellow!' and the troll shrank to the size of a mouse and disappeared under the shed. Kabir was in a state.

In fact, he became hysterical and started running in circles screaming, 'HELP ME HELP ME HELP ME!' and that's when Stink decided to shrink him too.

'YELLOW!' she cried and **BOOM!**

HELP ME!

HELP ME!

HELP!

HELP!

Kabir shrank.

Now I became hysterical. 'Stink, why did you do that?!'

'Because he was hurting my little ears!' she said.

I picked up mouse-sized

Kabir (to stop the foxes from eating him) and held him tight.

'Stink! I can't believe you shrank my best friend!'

'Temporarily,' she said.

I had to get a grip on this situation, which, by the way, Sophie was still finding very funny. The troll was nowhere to be seen so I took mini-Kabir up to the tree house to keep him safe. Stink came too, clinging to my shoulder.

It was Sophie who worked out how to calm Kabir down. She's got a hamster (Joan) that she loves and she basically put Kabir in her lap and stroked him like she strokes Joan: hard and without a break.

There, there!

Nice Kabir!

Good boy!

It looked painful, but it worked because soon Kabir shut up.

Once he was breathing normally, I knelt down and explained as well as I could what was going on. Here's a shortened version.

'My birthday . . . blah blah . . . rubbish present . . . fairy door . . . Stink . . . nuggets . . . blah blah . . . good deed . . . Najin . . . troll . . . you . . . eaten.'

And that's when Kabir grew back to his normal size. It happened in the blink of the eye. One moment mini-Kabir was sitting on my sister's lap, then BLINK a normal-sized Kabir was sitting on my sister's lap. She tried to keep him there, being stroked . . .

Good boy

. . . but he rolled off.

'So where's this fairy?' he said, nervously (because I'd told him all about her biting and wand prodding).

'On my shoulder watching you,' I said.

'Hello,' said Stink.

Kabir's eyes went big and wide and his mouth fell open, but he recovered quickly.

'Oh, yeah, it's a fairy,' he said with a shrug. 'I used to have a fairy only it was bigger.'

Before I go on, you need to know about . . . KABIR'S LIES.

My friend Kabir is a liar. He always claims he's got the best, biggest, newest, rarest of everything. You might think it's bad having a friend who makes stuff up, but if you think that, you're wrong. Kabir's lies are so MASSIVE they're funny. Here are some of his best ones. I've put a truth in there as well. See if you can find it.

1. It might look like Kabir's dad is a plumber, but he actually works for the F.B.I. installing spyware in taps.

2. The same spy-plumber dad once got on to *The Voice*, but his F.B.I. bosses wouldn't let him take part because it would have revealed his face (and voice) to the nation.

3. Kabir was once doing a wheelie on his bike when he hit a tree and knocked the tree over and it hit an old lady.

4. He found a black widow spider in a bag of grapes.

6. His mum's mobile phone is made of solid gold.

7. He trapped his hand in the door at the library and got ALL his fingers chopped off. Luckily his Mum put them in a bag of frozen chips which kept them fresh until they could be sewn back on. That's why Kabir never eats fish fingers and chips.

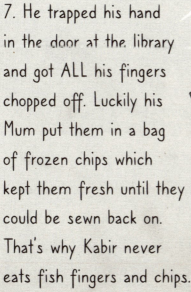

8. He was down at the skate-park working on his moves when Dwayne 'The Rock' Johnson went past walking his dog. The dog ran away, but Kabir caught it by skating really fast downhill. When he gave the dog back, The Rock said, 'Thanks, Kid.' (Which is why Kabir thinks everyone should call him The Kid.)

9. He was on a plane with two escaped snakes.

KABIR # ULLAH

10. His middle name is the symbol #

   (The true story is the one about the tree and the old lady, but it was a very small tree in a pot at a garden centre and the old lady was fine.)

I seriously doubted that Kabir had ever had a fairy, but I didn't get the chance to say this because that's when Mum turned up.

'Wow! You've done a good job on the garden,' she said. 'It's a bit rough around the edges, but nothing a bit of pruning won't sort out.'

Then she took a struggling Sophie off for her lunch. This was good. I needed to find that troll and I couldn't babysit and troll hunt at the same time.

'Right, you two,' said Stink, flying between me and Kabir and prodding us with her wand.

'We need to find that troll before it eats anything it shouldn't.'

'Like what?' I said.

'You,' she replied.

Nervously, Kabir and I started to look for the troll in Najin's half-empty garden.

I was peering under the shed when I heard a whiny voice say, 'You got LEAVES on OUR lawn!'

'Our Dad's going to KILL you!' came a second equally whiny voice.

That's right. The Budgen Twins were back.

17. Rafts and Chocolate

Poppy and Fin were once again leaning over the garden fence.

'Come and see what you've done!' said Poppy.

Stink dived into my hair then Kabir and I peered over the fence. Sure enough, a few leaves were scattered across their immaculate lawn. Considering how the troll tore through Najin's garden this was pretty amazing.

'It's some leaves. So what?' said Kabir. 'A troll just ate me.'

Poppy and Fin did identical expressions of disbelief mixed with disgust.

'You are such a liar, Kabir Ullah,' said Fin.

Now this annoyed me. Although what Fin said was true, right now The Kid was telling 100% the truth. Plus Kabir doesn't mean to lie. He just loves telling good stories. PLUS he's my best friend and only *I* get to say he's a liar. I opened my mouth to defend him, but Kabir got there first.

I'm not lying and there's a fairy in Danny's hair.

Just then a voice hissed from somewhere above my ear . . .

Make him shut up! Those two will tell grown-ups about me and then there will be magic goo and then I'll be DEAD!

HA HA! Good one, Kabir. Oh look she's getting ready to fly out of my hair and shrink you and almost certainly bite you because she feels VERY strongly about being kept a secret!

Got it!

Can you two stop being weird for one second AND stop putting leaves on our lawn. I'm going to have a chocolate-themed birthday party, remember?

This was the moment that Kabir decided to start being sarcastic. Along with lying, this is something else he's great at doing.

'Ooooh, some leaves! Quick, call the police,' he said, then he got out his phone and pretended to dial 999. 'Hello,' he said, into his phone.

'I'd like to report a serious crime. There are three illegal leaves on the Budgens' lawn. You'll send someone round straight away? Great. Make sure they're your very best detective. In fact, maybe send three detectives, one for each leaf. Thanks. See you soon!' Then he put his phone away and grinned at Poppy and Fin.

Up in my hair, Stink giggled. Poppy and Fin didn't.

Fin growled.

GRRR!

Poppy went red and made her eyes the size of small pebbles. 'We're getting the garden ready for my chocolate-themed birthday party tomorrow and we can't have leaves floating around. They might clog up the chocolate fountain!'

'Yeah!' said Fin. 'Or stick

to the varnish on the *Phantom Rip*.'

'What's the *Phantom Rip*?' I asked.

'That's the *Phantom Rip*!' said Fin pointing towards their patio.

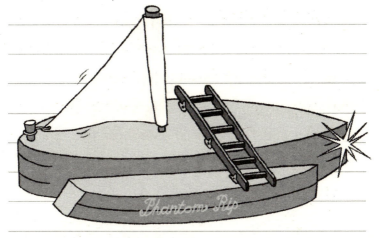

Poppy whipped a flyer out of her pocket and dangled it over the fence. 'Tomorrow, while I'm having my chocolate-themed birthday party,' (YES, WE GET IT, POPPY BUDGEN. YOUR PARTY IS CHOCOLATE-THEMED) 'Fin is having his birthday treat. He's made that raft with Mum and they're going to enter and win Mumbles-on-Sea's Wacky Raft Race.'

A snarl of rage made me turn round.

'What the flipping heck is going on out here?!' Professor Najin was glaring at us from her patio. 'Has my garden become some sort of youth club? What next? Are you going to have a disco? Are you going to dance and drink fizzy pop?' She stomped towards us. In a flash, Fin and Poppy vanished behind the fence. Their flyer floated to the ground.

'Where has this extra boy come from?' Najin asked, jabbing a finger at Kabir. 'And who dropped this litter in my garden!' She snatched up the flyer.

And that's the moment Stink decided to fire off a new spell – Mauve – and a tail popped out of the back of Najin's shorts.

'Stink!' I hissed.
'Sorry,' she said. 'I was aiming for the twins.'

18. The Race

Amazingly, Professor Najin didn't notice her new tail (which was yellow and fluffy, a bit like a golden retriever's) because she was gazing at the flyer.

'Fix the tail!' I hissed to Stink, then I rushed forwards. My plan was to distract Najin while Stink reversed the spell by shouting, 'Evuam!' Only Najin didn't need distracting.

Her tail was wagging and her eyes were glued to the flyer:

CALLING ALL SALTY OLD SEA DOGS!

SHIVER ME TIMBERS, MUMBLES-ON-SEA IS HAVING A WACKY RAFT RACE!

SET SAIL FROM THE FISHING CLUB AT NOON, SATURDAY 28TH AUGUST.

ALL HANDMADE SEA-WORTHY CRAFTS ELIGIBLE. FIRST PRIZE: AN INFLATABLE SUP BOARD.

YO HO HO AND THE BEST OF LUCK, SHIPMATES!

Waasss SUP!!

'A SUP board,' I said, reading over her shoulder. 'I'd love one of those . . .'

'Already got one,' muttered Kabir, half-heartedly.

'Pah!' said Najin then she stuffed the flyer in her pocket, strode to the very end of her semi-empty garden and kicked open a gate in the fence.

I'm starting to realise that Najin does everything violently. Her and Stink have a lot in common.

Speaking of Stink, she shot out of my hair, pointed her wand and cried, *'Evuam!'* Najin's tail vanished in a puff of blue smoke.

'Oi!' Najin bellowed like an army major. 'Disco kids! Follow me! There's something I want to show you.'

Stink squirmed into my hair as we followed Najin through the gate. This is what we saw:

Sometimes I forget that there's a river running along the bottom of our gardens. It leads to the fishing club then out to sea. It's one of the reasons Mum and Dad bought our house, but ever since we moved in our gate has been permanently locked because Sophie can't be trusted around water (or sweets, or animals, or mobile phones, or stairs, or jelly, or scissors, or chewing gum, or toothpaste).

'What's that lump of junk?' said Kabir, pointing at the boat.

'It's a hippotottymouse,' whispered Stink with great confidence. 'I saw a picture of it in *Humanyland for Beginners*, chapter six, Scary Animals.'

Humanyland for Begginers
6. SCARY Animals!!

The Hippotottymouse

Najin glared at Kabir. 'Did you just call the *Hot Rod* a LUMP OF JUNK? I'll tell you who's a lump of junk, boy. YOU ARE!' And with that she shoved him in the stomach.

'*Hot Rod* was the finest yacht to sail these waters,' said Najin gazing at the, well, lump of junk poking out of the water. 'She would shoot along the waves faster than a cat who's sat on a wasp.'

'What happened to her?' I asked.

'Jasper Budgen is what happened to her,' said Najin, her eyes flicking to the Budgens' house. 'He complained that she caused a racket clanking in the wind. Then, the next day, I came out and found her like this. Murdered . . . I've got no proof that he did it. Just what my gut tells me . . . and the fact that the next day he was whistling and that man *never* whistles.'

'Why don't you pull it out of the river and fix it?' asked Kabir.

'Do you think I'm made of money?' Najin snapped back, then her voice softened and she said, 'She really was the most magnificent vessel.'

I don't know about Kabir, but I felt sorry for Najin just then. All day she sat watching videos about sailing, but she used to go sailing for real.

For a moment, I wondered if me and Slink could fix the boat . . . Najin might teach me and Kabir how to sail and then I'd get a great tan and finally learn to dive and maybe even find a sunken ship!

'Hey, Stink,' I whispered. Her face appeared upside down in front of my face. 'Can you do some magic to mend Najin's boat?'

She gave me a withering look. 'No, of course I can't mend Najin's boat. I'd need a unicorn-horn wand to do magic like that. Mine's made out of witch nail clippings and pixie hair all mashed together.'

Suddenly Najin spun round and Stink disappeared back into my hair.

'Garden's still a mess,' Najin said, then she stomped through the gate and across her garden.

And that's when I remembered we were supposed to be looking for a troll.

19. Blue Nose Day

It was Kabir who discovered that the troll had escaped from the garden.

'Uh oh, troll hole,' he said, pointing at the fence.

'Stink!' I said, shaking her out of my hair. 'The troll's got out and it looks like it's grown back to its normal size. What do we do now?'

She yawned and fluttered in and out of the troll hole.

'Dunno,' she said. 'Go and look for it?'

So that's what we did. To be honest, the troll wasn't difficult to track down.

Prof. Najin's house

'This definitely isn't doing a good deed,' I said to Stink. 'It's doing a *bad* deed. You'll probably get your wings taken away for this.'

Stink was sitting on my shoulder and I felt her shudder. 'Then I'd have to *walk*,' she said.

'I'd rather die than walk. Walking's for total idiots.'

Like total idiots, me and Kabir walked on through Mumbles-on-Sea, following the troll's trail of destruction. When we got to the park the trail went cold. Well almost . . .

'What are those dollops on the slide?' said Kabir.

'Troll poos,' said Stink. 'Actually, can you collect them for me? One plop is worth a tuppenny nugget in Fairyland.'

I was about to tell Stink that there was no way I was touching troll poo when Kabir said, 'Budgen alert!'

Poppy and Fin were striding towards us each clutching a stripy paper bag. Stink shot into my hair.

'Guess what's in here?' said Poppy.

'Dead mermaids?' suggested Stink.

Luckily the twins didn't hear her.

'SWEETS!' Poppy cried with a greedy smile.
'Loads and loads of SWEETS! Dad gave us
twenty pounds to spend on pick 'n' mix to dip in
the chocolate fountain at my chocolate-themed
birthday party. Do you want to see them?'

Honestly? Yes I did. Who wouldn't want to see
twenty pounds' worth of pick 'n' mix?

In case you're curious.
This is what it looks
like.

Me and Kabir
both had a good
look in the bags.
Even Stink had a
peek. The sweets
smelled amazing and
I was sure the twins were
going to offer us one especially when Kabir said,
'I love giant jazzies. They're my favourites.'

'Yeah? Me too,' said Fin, shoving one in his mouth.

Suddenly a small high voice rang out from inside my hair.

You dropped one!

'What did you say?' said Fin.

I felt like I had no choice but to repeat what Stink had just said. And for some reason I thought it would be a good idea to imitate her voice.

'You dropped one,' I squeaked.

Fin's eyes narrowed suspiciously as he glanced at the floor. His eyes settled on a bright blue troll dropping. Quick as a flash, his hand shot out and he snatched it up. 'Five second rule,' he said as he popped it in his mouth.

And that's when I realised I'd just got Fin Budgen to eat troll poo. My head vibrated as Stink shook with silent laughter.

Fin happily munched on the sweet, sorry, *troll poo*. And then, in the blink of an eye, his nose turned blue.

'Fin, your nose is blue!' said Poppy.

'No it isn't,' he replied, uncertainly.

But Poppy was already marching across the park yelling. 'Yes it is! You've got a blue nose and I'm telling Mum!'

'STINK!' I said, the second they were gone. 'We made him eat troll poo and now he's got a blue nose. That is NOT a good deed!'

'I don't know,' said Kabir. 'It kind of *is*.'

Stink wasn't bothered. She just dropped down on to my shoulder and sucked on a jelly bean that

she'd somehow nicked from the Budgens' bag.
'Don't worry about it,' she said. 'There's loads
of kids eating them.'

And that's when I realised that the playground
was full of multi-coloured-nosed children. No
one could resist the troll poo!

For the next ten minutes, Kabir and I ran
around snatching troll poo out of children's hands
and shoving them in our pockets.

Stink was thrilled. 'That's almost three
nuggets' worth of poo you've got there,' she said.

'Listen, Stink,' I said. 'How long do the noses
last for? Please tell me the colour will go away.'

'Yeah, probably . . . maybe,' she said.

'Er, Danny,' said Kabir, pulling on my T-shirt. 'I reckon we should get out of here. Things are about to kick off.'

A girl with a green nose was pointing at me and my bulging pockets of droppings. She was with two dads and both of them, I noticed, were massive.

'OI! I want a word with you, sweet boy!' said the biggest dad, then he started to jog towards me.

'My dad could destroy him,' said Kabir, quickly followed by, 'RUN!'

We started to leg it across the park.

'Why don't you skate?' I shouted at Kabir.

'Nah, mate. Couldn't leave you on your own, could I?'

Stink decided to help us escape by sticking her head out of my hair and giving us a commentary on what the most massive dad was up to.

He's running really, really, fast!

He looks as muscly as a mermaid and they're so strong they can crack coconuts open with their todds.

I'll do some magic to slow him down. PINK!

In a flash, a cloud of pink smoke surrounded me and I couldn't see a thing. 'Did it work?' I shouted, then I tripped over a bin.

'Definitely!' said Stink. 'I disguised you with pink smoke. He can't see you, can he?'

But just then a hairy hand reached into the smoke, trying to grab hold of me.

'This way, mate!' yelled Kabir and he pulled me towards a gap in a hedge that was definitely too small for a massive dad to squeeze through. We bundled through then legged it all the way back to Najin's garden.

I only felt safe when we were up in the tree house. At least, kind of safe, because the troll was still out there eating stuff and leaving its nose-altering poos all over the place.

Stink tumbled out of my hair and started fluttering around the tree house. 'Is it just me,' she said, 'or was that the BEST fun you've had in ages? Did you see Fin stick the troll poo in his mouth? HA HA! So funny. And that dad looked like he wanted to kill you, Danny!'

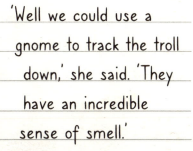

'It's definitely just you,' I said. 'That was terrifying. Stink, we have GOT to catch the troll. How are we going to do it?'

'Well, there is one thing we could try . . .'

'What?' I said, desperately.

But she shook her head and said, 'No, it's too risky.'

Please, Stink, I'll try anything!

'Well we could use a gnome to track the troll down,' she said. 'They have an incredible sense of smell.'

'Brilliant!' I said. 'Where can we get a gnome from?'

She landed on the floor and started pacing up and down. 'Now *that's* an interesting question. Gnomes are *rare*, Danny. Some say they can be found in the Crystal Mines, deep below the poisoned waters of the Luna River*.

It's a one-hundred-day journey by boat to reach the entrance to the caves, that's if you survive the ear-nesting eels and the nose-bitey sprites. Plus, to get to the entrance you have to negotiate the maze of lava that lies beneath the Castle of Hair and Teeth, and *that's* guarded by the Dragon-Who-Eats-Kids and she can hear an ant's heart beating

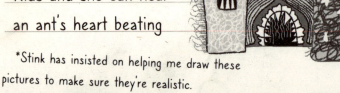

*Stink has insisted on helping me draw these pictures to make sure they're realistic.

twenty miles away, so, you know, getting a gnome *isn't* impossible, but it would involve an epic journey, and, assuming we all go, not all of us would return.' She pointed at Kabir. 'You'd be the first to go.'

'What? Why?' he asked, looking offended.

Because Danny's got me, his very own fairy, to protect him.

'Yeah, well I've got two fairies,' said Kabir.

'Whatever,' said Stink. 'What I'm trying to say is that finding a gnome is going to be very difficult indeed.'

'Hang on,' I said. 'Hasn't your brother got a gnome?'

'Oh yeah!' she said. 'Ellis. I'll go back home and steal, I mean, borrow him.'

Diary, it is now bedtime and once again Stink has gone back through the fairy door to Fairyland. This time she took Tony with her, so she could 'get back quicker with Ellis'.

I'm going to try and sleep, but it's hard to relax when you know there's a sweet-pooping troll loose in your town and it's all your fault.

But I'm not giving up. It was me and my sarcastic rhyme that brought Stink and then the troll here so it's me who's got to sort everything out.

I just hope Ellis is up to the job.

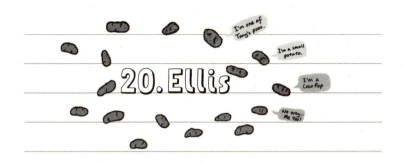

20. Ellis

When I woke up, I found a small, naked gnome sitting on my chest. Luckily for me, he had a VERY bushy beard.

I wasn't that surprised. Since Stink turned up nothing much surprises me, but I did insist that he put on some clothes.

It turned out Ellis was the same size as Sophie's Build-A-Bear so he had several outfits to choose from.

'Isn't he weird,' said Stink eyeing Ellis from a distance. 'My brother thinks he's *IT* wandering around with his pet gnome, but I just think he's weird.'

Stink was lying. She obviously loved Ellis and couldn't take her eyes off him. Except for his beard I didn't think he was that special . . . that was until I offered him a piece of toast.

The little dude is all teeth and beard! It's like a shark and Santa have had a baby.

Sophie wandered into my room with a bowl of dry Coco Pops (she says milk smells like Mum) and started feeding Ellis grains of puffed rice one by one. Each time his mouth snapped open she laughed like mad.

As soon as Kabir turned up we went next door to Najin's tree house which has become our headquarters.

'We're like the Justice League or the Avengers or something,' said Kabir.

I looked at Kabir, Stink and the gnome. I've always wanted to be a part of a crime-fighting team, but I never imagined it would contain a boy who pretends to skate, a fairy and a gnome wearing a Princess Jasmine costume.

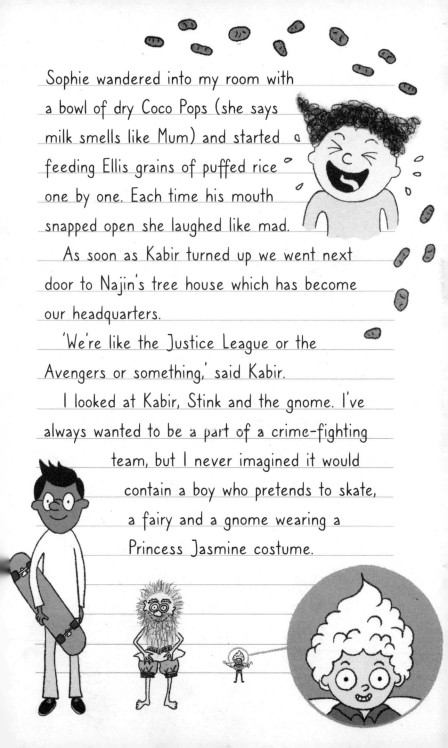

But then I realised that this *was* my crime-fighting team and it was time for me to start acting like their leader.

'Right,' I said, putting Ellis down. 'Off you go! Find the troll!'

He sat there in his Princess Jasmine costume staring up at me.

'Why's he just sitting there?' I asked Stink.

'You need to pay him, obviously,' she said. 'Gnomes don't do anything for free. Fandango has to pay him a nugget a week to be his pet.'

'What does he want paying with?' I asked.

'I don't know,' said Stink. 'I'll ask him.' Then she pulled a little book out of her pocket that had 'Learn to Speak Gnome in 40 Moons' written on the front. After a lot of flicking backward and forward she said . . .

Sooty gnu ripputy chubbit?

Ellis looked around the tree house, taking everything in. Then he pointed a gnarled finger at Kabir's skateboard and said, '*Herty mutch luff.*'

'What does that mean?' I asked Stink.

Once again she flicked through her book. 'He said, "I want his chariot".'

'No way!' said Kabir.

'Deal,' I said.

Ellis reached out and wrenched the skateboard from Kabir's hands.

'So how does he sniff out the troll?' I asked.

'By following its scent,' said Stink and she held up one of the troll's sweetie shaped poos.

Immediately Ellis's nostrils started twitching.

'Right,' I said, realising that Ellis was like a sniffer dog. 'Wherever he goes, we'll follow him and the second he finds the troll Stink will hit them with her Yellow spell and shrink them both down. Got it?'

Kabir and Stink nodded, and suddenly I felt confident. I felt like the leader of a crime-fighting team who was fully in control.

As we climbed down from the tree house I had a spring in my step. In fact, I was enjoying feeling like the leader of a crime-fighting team so much I thought I'd do another speech.

'This is it,' I said, as I held the troll poo out to Ellis. 'Get ready to run, guys, because it is troll hunting time!'

Ellis leaned forward. His big nostrils quivered over the poo and then he shot out of the garden on the skateboard so fast he was just a blur of beard, wheels and turquoise hareem pants.

21. The Chocolate Fountain

Stink looked furious. 'Danny, what were you thinking? You NEVER let a gnome loose unless it's wearing its tracking device.' She pulled a bell out of her pocket and jingled it in my face. 'EVERYONE knows that!'

Yeah, Danny! Why'd you do that?

Stink never told me!

I was about to then you let him go. Oh well . . . Bye, bye troll.

What do you mean?

Well, Ellis is going to find him and eat him, isn't he?

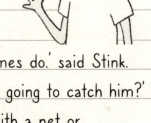

What?! Why?

'Because that's what gnomes do.' said Stink. 'How did *you* think Ellis was going to catch him?'

'Gently, in his hands or with a net or something,' I said.

'Nope,' said Stink. 'If we're not there when Ellis finds that troll then he's going to catch him with his big sharp teeth and swallow him whole.'

She said all this as if it was my fault. As if *I'd* been the one to suggest using a gnome to track the troll down, gone and got it from Fairyland and given it some troll poo to sniff.

Actually, I did do that last thing, but I didn't do any of the other stuff.

But I realised there was no point in arguing with Stink. If we didn't find that troll before Ellis then I'd be an accessory to troll murder and I didn't want to be an accessory to murdering anything.

At school, I've only ever had my name on the grey cloud once and that was in Year Two when Kabir and I drew moustaches on each other using Miss Shepherd's Sharpies.

'Stink!' I said, picking her up and holding her in front of my face. 'Where could the troll be? We've got to find it before Ellis does.'

Just then Professor Najin came into the garden with a bucket of scraps for her wormery.

'What's going on out here?' she said suspiciously.

'Nothing,' I said, hiding Stink in my hands.
Quickly we retreated behind a big bush.
'Stink!' I said, giving her a shake. 'Think!
Where would a troll go? What do they like?'

She screwed up her tiny face then, after a lot of uuumming and aaahhhing she said, 'Chocolate. Trolls love chocolate!'

And that's when we remembered Poppy's

Chocolate!

CHOCOLATE-THEMED BIRTHDAY PARTY!

22. Willy Wonka

We peered into the Budgens' garden.

Well, Kabir and I did, and Stink flew up and sat on the fence.

'What is *that*?' said Stink.

'*That* is a chocolate-themed birthday party,' I told her.

The *Phantom Rip* was gone from the patio – I guess Fin and his mum were taking part in the Wacky Raft Race – and in its place were loads of girls, sweets and chocolates.

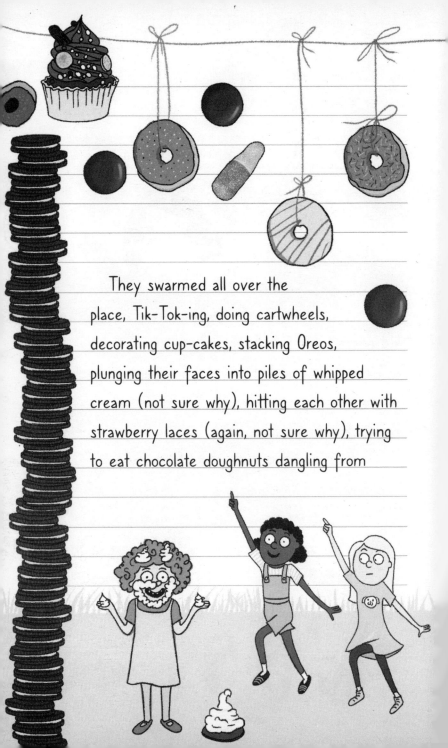

They swarmed all over the place, Tik-Tok-ing, doing cartwheels, decorating cup-cakes, stacking Oreos, plunging their faces into piles of whipped cream (not sure why), hitting each other with strawberry laces (again, not sure why), trying to eat chocolate doughnuts dangling from

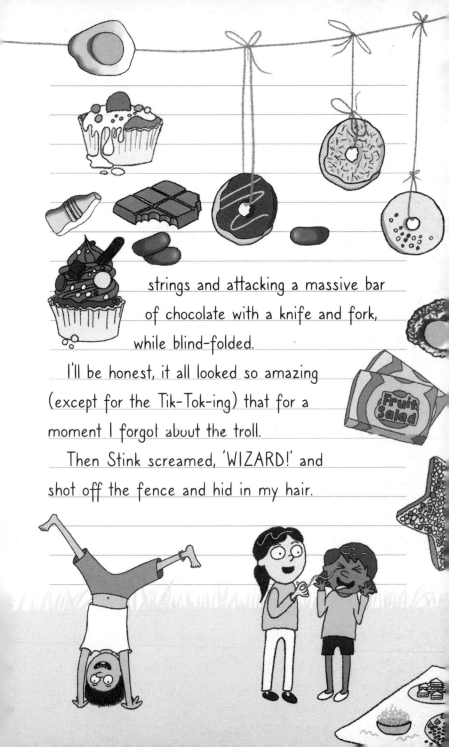

strings and attacking a massive bar
of chocolate with a knife and fork,
while blind-folded.

I'll be honest, it all looked so amazing
(except for the Tik-Tok-ing) that for a
moment I forgot about the troll.

Then Stink screamed, 'WIZARD!' and
shot off the fence and hid in my hair.

It wasn't a wizard. It was Jasper Budgen, the twins dad, who had come into the garden dressed as Willy Wonka.

'I hope you're having fun at my chocolate factory, girls,' he boomed. 'It's nearly time for the chocolate fountain!'

Suddenly, a warm splat landed on my cheek. Automatically my tongue went out to lick it and I tasted chocolate. SPLAT. More chocolate landed on my nose and chin.

'Oh no,' said Kabir, nudging me and pointing at a chocolate fountain arranged on a table at the bottom of the garden. It was obviously the highlight of the party and Jasper Budgen had strung a rope across the garden to keep the girls away. Perhaps that's why no one had noticed the troll.

I think the best word to describe what it was doing is *frolicking*.

That troll was frolicking in melted chocolate like the happiest chocolate-loving troll in the universe.

'I'll get him back,' said Stink then she burst out of my hair and went fluttering across the garden like a drunk sparrow. She *really* needed new wings.

'Go on, Stink. Go on Stink!' I whispered under my breath.

At the top of the garden Jasper Budgen (AKA Willy Wonka) was getting the girls pumped about the chocolate fountain.

Have I got a surprise for you, my little Oompa Loompas! My most wondrous invention yet – a magical chocolate fountain and you won't believe the secret ingredient I popped in the mixture.

'It's a smelly troll,' said Kabir.

I gripped the top of the fence, willing Stink to hurry up and reach the troll, but her wings were so rubbish she kept dropping down in the sky.

Finally she reached the chocolate fountain. But she didn't take out her wand or shout, 'Yellow!' to shrink the troll. Instead she cried, 'YIPPEEEEE!' and dived head first into the top tier of melted chocolate. Then she started frolicking just like the troll, swimming up and down through the thick chocolate and squirting it out of her mouth.

Now there was a troll *and* a fairy in Poppy Budgen's chocolate fountain.

And Jasper Budgen had decided it was time to unleash the girls. He untied the rope and called out, 'Who wants to dip some magical sweeties into gooey chocolate?'

'Me! Me!' cried the girls as they threw down their Oreos, paper plates of cream, strawberry laces and icing bags and surged towards the bottom of the garden.

'What are we going to do?' hissed Kabir.

'*Yellow!*' I called over the fence, desperately hoping Stink would hear me and remember what she was supposed to be doing.

'What is going on here?' I turned round and found Professor Najin standing right behind me.

'Um . . . I'm shouting "Yellow" into the Budgens' garden,' I said.

'Good, that will annoy them,' she said, then she threw back her head and bellowed . . .

YELLOW!

It was so loud that Stink shot out of the gooey mixture. She took one look at the girls rushing towards her, whipped out her wand and screeched, 'YELLOW!'

A puff of green smoke exploded over the chocolate fountain and when it faded away the troll had gone. Presumably it was now tiny and swimming in the melted chocolate.

This was good because the girls were all crowded round the fountain and grabbing handfuls of pick 'n' mix . Any second now they were going to start dipping the sweets into the chocolate.

Someone had to go and get the troll out of the chocolate fountain, but Stink couldn't do it. Not only was she about the same size as the troll, her wings were so clogged up with chocolate she could barely fly. She drifted back towards us like a fat chocolate-covered bumble bee.

'Willy Wonka, I put my face in the chocolate!' cried Poppy.

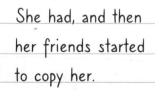

She had, and then her friends started to copy her.

If I didn't get that troll out
of there, one of the girls
might swallow the troll
and what would happen
when Stink's Yellow spell
wore off?

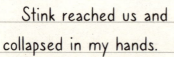

Growing troll

Stink reached us and
collapsed in my hands.

'Too much chocolate,' she gasped.

'Can you do another spell?' I said, but she
groaned, clutched her stomach and shook her
head.

'Look, now I'm *drinking* the chocolate!' yelled
Poppy.

It was time for Danny Todd to act.

I thrust a sticky Stink into Kabir's hands and
said, 'Look after my fairy.'

Then I glanced over my shoulder to see what
Professor Najin was up to. She had climbed on
top of her wormery and her head was stuck
inside one of the water butts. Good. That meant

she wouldn't see what I was about to do which was . . .

climb over the garden fence and into the Budgens' garden with no plan at all.

Thud. I landed on the grass and crouched like a tiger.

Creepy, creepy, stealthy, stealthy. Like a panther, I crept  towards the chocolate-guzzling girls.

Then I froze, poised (like a jaguar), ready to pounce.

Then Poppy screamed, 'DAD! Danny Todd's in our garden!'

And I realised that I looked more like a weirdo than a jaguar.

'What are you up to?' asked Jasper, eyeballing me from under his top hat.

I had to think fast. I had to come up with a believable reason for a) why I was in his garden and b) why he should let me stick my hands in his daughter's chocolate fountain.

And this is what I said.

Kabir just threw a LEGO man in your chocolate fountain.

(Unbelievable: like me, Kabir can't throw with any accuracy)

I don't want it to ruin Poppy's party.

(Unbelievable: Poppy is horrible; I don't care what happens to her party)

'I'm just going to find it.
(Believable)

Reaching for the chocolate fountain, I tried to dodge round Jasper Budgen.

'Oh no you don't, young man,' he said, blocking my way. 'Your hands could have been anywhere.

If what you say is true, then I'll find the LEGO man.'

'NO!' bellowed Kabir from behind the fence.

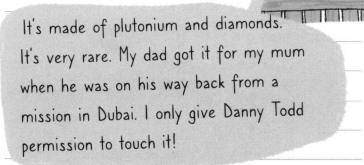

It's made of plutonium and diamonds. It's very rare. My dad got it for my mum when he was on his way back from a mission in Dubai. I only give Danny Todd permission to touch it!

A classic Kabir lie. It was long and detailed and it gave me just enough time to duck round Jasper Budgen, plunge my hands into the chocolate and find the troll. It was easy. It was starting to grow.

Quickly, I stuffed it up my T-shirt.

Then all hell broke loose.

Girls and Willy Wonka tried to catch me. The troll squirmed and scratched. Stink (who had flown back across the garden and was now in

my hair), screamed, 'Bite them and run, Danny!
BITE THEM AND RUN!'

I wasn't biting anyone, but I did run and
because I was covered in melted chocolate
I managed to squirm away from all the hands
trying to grab me.

Growing
troll

Kabir helped me to scramble over the fence
and I fell on to Najin's lawn, panting and trying
to keep the hairy troll inside my T-shirt.

Suddenly a top hat appeared over the fence,
followed by Jasper Budgen's angry face. 'Your
parents are going to hear about this, Danny
Todd!' he hissed before tipping his hat and
vanishing from sight.

23. The Wormery

'Shrink it down! Shrink it down!' I yelled to Stink. The troll had clamped its mouth on to my tummy button and was sucking with all its might.

'I can't,' she said, dangling over my forehead to get a better view. 'My wand needs time to charge back up again.'

'Mate,' said Kabir. 'I think it's going to suck your insides out.'

'Help me!' I cried, then Kabir and even Stink tried to pull the troll off my stomach.

It detached with a SLURP!, shot out of their hands and landed on top of the wormery. Luckily, Najin still had her head stuck in one of the butts and didn't have a clue that a hairy chocolatey beast was sitting next to her.

'Get that troll!' yelled Stink, but before we could move, a whirling ball of beard and sequins came skateboarding into the garden.

Ellis was back. He had followed the troll's trail around town and it had led him all the way back here. And the exercise had made him hungry.

He jumped off the skateboard which shot across the garden. Then he caught sight of the troll and went running towards the wormery with his jaws flung wide open.

He was going to eat the troll! Even if he

missed, he would almost certainly sink his teeth into Najin's sensible shorts-covered bottom.

'Go! Go! Go!' yelled Stink from up in my hair.

Kabir and I started to run. Kabir reached the wormery just before me and threw himself on top of the troll, stuffing him inside one of the water butts.

But Ellis was still coming, his teeth glittering in the sun and saliva drooling from his mouth.

'Do something, Danny!' yelled Stink.

I couldn't stop Ellis, but I could move the wormery. I gave it a shove and it slid on top of the abandoned skateboard and started rolling down the garden.

'What did you do that for?' yelled Stink.

'I don't know. It seemed like a good idea! Can't you do your Yellow spell on Ellis?!'

A small puff of smoke exploded over my head. 'Sorry, wand's still empty. You'd better get after them. Ellis is ready to bite!'

I charged down the garden and soon Ellis and I were racing side by side, both of us trying to reach the wormery first.

Ellis was hungry for troll.

But I knew it was my job to protect the troll (and Kabir and Najin).

I ran faster than I had ever run in my life. I ran so fast that I didn't even know what my legs were doing. I ran so fast my teeth chattered.

And I beat Ellis to the wormery.

   With one giant leap I landed next to Kabir.
The wormery picked up speed. Ellis snarled,
gnashed his teeth, then jumped after us.

   Then, just as the wormery smashed through
the fence at the bottom of the garden, Ellis
sank his teeth into one of the water butts.

   And that's how we splashed down in the river.

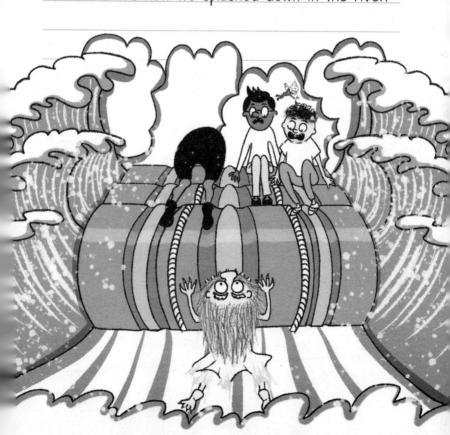

24. THE PHANTOM RIP

When Najin pulled her head out of the water butt she couldn't believe her eyes.

What are you lot doing on my wormery?

Why are we in the river?

Why's a car just floated past . . . and a giant banana . . . and a unicorn?

I decided to skip the first two questions and just focus on number three.

'They're all wacky rafts,' I said. 'Look, they're sailing towards the fishing club. That's where the wacky raft race begins.'

Najin's eyes went starey. She stared at all the wacky rafts bobbing along in the water and she stared at Kabir and me. Stink shot into my hair just in time and the troll was still trapped inside one of the water butts. Ellis was hidden too, just under the water, but he was making his presence felt. Still desperate to get at the troll he was pedalling his hairy feet like mad. He'd turned the wormery into a speed boat and we were shooting through the water, banging against rafts and spraying water all over the place.

'Oi!' shouted an angry voice. 'Keep your raft under control.'

At that moment, Ellis must have decided to take a break because we slowed down and found ourselves bobbing alongside the *Phantom Rip*.

'I said,' came the angry voice again,

KEEP YOUR RAFT UNDER CONTROL!

The voice belonged to Esther Budgen, and she was standing, legs apart, on the Phantom Rip.

She was wearing an outfit of deck shoes, white trousers and a blue stripy top.

'You scratched our paintwork!' cried Fin (who was also wearing an outfit of deck shoes, white trousers and a blue stripy top).

Stare, went Najin, taking in their sleek vessel and their matching peaked caps.

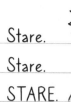

Stare.

Stare.

STARE.

Perhaps this unnerved Esther because suddenly she whipped a piece of paper out of her pocket and said, 'Anyway, you can't enter the race. Rule number four says, "All vessels must be captained by a responsible adult with experience of sailing". No offence, Professor Najin, but that can't be you, can it? Your boat sank.'

Najin narrowed her eyes. 'It was your husband who sank my boat and you know it!'

Esther gasped. 'You've no evidence of that!'

'Yeah,' said Fin. 'You can't prove Dad drilled holes in it with his cordless Makita combi drill!'

'SHUT UP, Fin!' hissed Esther Budgen.

By now we had joined the clump of wacky rafts bobbing around by the fishing club. A rope was slung between two buoys marking the start of the race. The riverbank was packed with a cheering crowd.

It felt exciting to be part of a race, even if we weren't supposed to be in it.

'Anyway,' said Esther, 'you can't enter the race because your raft doesn't have a sail and you don't have any paddles. I made our paddles from a Victorian dresser, but you don't have any paddles at all. In fact, your raft is a disgrace.'

'Ooooh!' whispered Stink's voice in my ear. 'I HATE her!'

I think we all hated Esther Budgen just then, but there wasn't much we could do about it because at that moment a horn blasted, the rope dropped and all the rafts surged forwards. Well, all of them except ours.

Within seconds the wormery had been left behind.

Najin watched them go, a look of desperate longing on her face.

I turned away and shook Stink out of my hair and into my hands.

'Stink,' I whispered. 'Is there any magic you can do to make this raft move? Can you conjure up a paddle or a sail?'

She pulled out her wand, but her shoulders sagged. She looked as crestfallen as Najin. 'Danny, my magic is rubbish. Fandango's been telling me that for years and he's right. I can make foxes change colour and cut down one blade of grass at a time, but that's it. If Fandango was here he would turn Ellis into a rocket, but I can't even turn him into a plank of wood that we can use as a paddle!'

I gave her a little shake. 'At least you can *do* some magic,' I said. 'I can't do any. Plus, I've only seen a few of your spells. Green Seventeen cut the grass in half – that was a good spell – so what happens if you do Green One or Two or Three?'

Her eyes went very big.

Bad stuff happens, Danny, very bad stuff . . .

25. The Bad Stuff

By now, Kabir and Najin were on their knees trying to paddle us back to shore.

But I hadn't given up yet. The sight of Fin's smug face as they sailed past us had put a fire in my belly.

I wanted us to win the wacky raft race, or, failing that, beat the *Phantom Rip*. Or, failing that, I'd just like to knock Fin and his mum into the sea and ruin their hats.

Bad stuff might be just what we needed.

'What sort of bad stuff?' I asked.

'Explosions,' said Stink. 'Green is an exploding spell and it is hard to do. Green One, Two, Three, Four, Five, Six, Seven, Eight, Nine, Ten,

Eleven, Twelve, Thirteen, Fourteen, Fifteen and Sixteen were all versions that didn't work. Apparently, I was getting my compounds mixed up with my atoms and my what-nots confused with my finky funkers. I don't know. I wasn't listening when my teacher told me off, but basically, I was making gas and breaking stuff. That's why I got chucked out of school and couldn't go to university.' She gives me a shifty look. 'I exploded my school, Danny. I filled it with gas and it went

BOOM! Fandango sorted it out with a reversing spell, but my teachers were really cross.'

I glanced at the back of the raft where Ellis

was still stuck to the wormery by his teeth. His beard trailed out behind him and his big feet were flipping backward and forward. If this was a boat, Ellis would be right where a motor would go . . . and motors need fuel . . . petrol or . . . GAS!

'What's your gassiest spell, Stink?' I said.

'Green Sixteen,' she said without hesitating. 'You could smell it for days. They called it S dot Tink's stinky stink . . . bit rude.'

I glanced at Professor Najin. She was still bent over the side of the raft, paddling like a dog.

I held Stink in front of my face.

Do it again, Stink. Hit Ellis with your Green Sixteen spell and make this baby fly!

She didn't take much persuading.

SWOOSH!

Out came her wand and she got into her spell stance. Then, without giving me any time to warn Najin or Kabir what was about to happen, she bellowed . . .

GREEN SIXTEEN!

And Ellis exploded.

26.
The Wacky Race

Even now I don't know exactly
where the gas escaped
from, all I know is that Ellis
become a turbo-charged
rocket that shot our wacky
raft through the water so fast
that my face looked like this:

Najin, Kabir and I clung on for our lives, as
the wormery sliced through the competition. Our
raft was like a cat that had sat on a thousand
wasps. It flew. It soared. It barely made contact
with the water as it bounced along. 'We must
have caught a rogue wave!' Professor Najin
cried. 'Hold on, boys!'

Budgens ←

Hot dog guy →

Us →

That's when I realised that we were heading straight towards the *Phantom Rip*.

Now I didn't like Esther and Fin Budgen, but that didn't mean I wanted to crash into them.

Luckily, Najin took control. She leaped to her feet and began to captain our vessel.

'You, boy!' She pointed at Kabir. 'Grab hold of that clew and reef the cringles.'

'You, other boy!' She pointed at me. 'Luff the boomvang windward!*' I think she wanted me to tighten a rope that was flapping around so I did.

*This might not be exactly what she said, but you get the idea.

Then Najin pulled off her anorak and tied it to the wormery to make a sail.

But we were still shooting towards the *Phantom Rip*.

'HARD TO PORT!' Najin yelled, leaning to the left.

We were seconds away from hitting the *Phantom Rip*.

'She means lean *LEFT*!' Stink squealed, yanking my hair to the left.

I grabbed Kabir and we threw ourselves to the left hand side of the wormery. Our wacky raft tipped and we shot past the *Phantom Rip*, missing it by a troll's whisker.

'DON'T YOU DARE OVERTAKE U-!' Esther Budgen's words were drowned out by a wave of water crashing down on her.

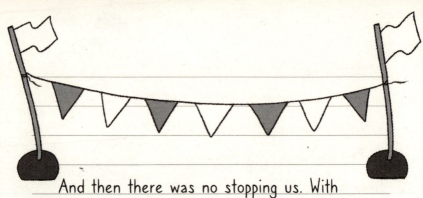

And then there was no stopping us. With Captain Najin at the helm, we dodged round the inflatable hotdog, shot ahead of the banana and dodged a giant baby. Soon we were at the head of the pack and racing towards the finishing line.

As we broke through the ribbon, another horn blasted and Najin, standing at the helm of the good ship *Wormery*, threw back her head and laughed.

And laughed . . .

. . . and laughed.

It was a surprising sound. I'd never heard a laugh coming out of her before. It was rough and cackly, like the laugh of a witch who

is also a part-time pirate.

It echoed across the sea and it made a flash of light explode on my shoulder.

Then this flew in front of my face. Stink had done her good deed. She'd earned her one hundred nuggets and got her Silver Bullets. She didn't need to save foxes or tidy up an entire garden. She just needed to make a grumpy old lady so happy that she laughed!

"YIPPEEEEEEE!!!" Stink cried and to the sound of Najin's cackles she looped higher and higher in the sky.

27. VICTORY!

Najin gazed at the horizon, a big grin on her face, while behind her a clean-up operation was taking place. Using her brand new wings, Stink darted around the wormery shrinking the troll and Ellis with one powerful blast of the Yellow spell. Just as Najin turned round, I tucked the squirming creatures into my pockets (keeping them apart so Ellis didn't eat the troll) and Stink dived into my hair.

Perhaps it was all the exercise and excitement, or maybe Stink's spell was extra good, but the troll and Ellis stayed shrunk and

relatively calm all the way through the prize-
giving ceremony.

I'm afraid, Esther and Fin Budgen weren't so
well behaved.

Just as the mayor was about to hang a
gleaming medal around Najin's neck they ran on
to the stage.

'They used an engine!' cried Esther Budgen,
jabbing a finger at us. 'And that breaks Rule
Eight which states: All wacky rafts must be
powered by wackiness, paddles and wind alone.
No motorised engines allowed.'

'Yeah!' added Fin. 'They *cheated!*'

The mayor paused, the medal dangling over
Najin's nail-scisssored hair.

'My wormery hasn't got a motor,' protested

Najin. 'It's just three water butts tied together with bungee cord.'

Kabir stuck up for her.

Yeah! It wasn't a motor that shot us through the water. It was a gnome's massive fart. The fairy that lives in Danny's hair did an exploding spell on the gnome and – BOOM – we flew!

For once Kabir was telling the truth, but luckily for me (and Stink who was trembling in my hair and hissing, 'If that lady sees me I will turn into fairy goo on your head, Danny!') no one believed him.

Instead, the mayor winked at Kabir and said, 'I'm sure that's what happened,' followed by, 'and we can see with our own eyes that Professor Najin's wacky raft doesn't have a motor.'

At that moment, the wormery was being placed next to the stage so that everyone could admire its simple yet effective construction.

The mayor fixed the Budgens with a fierce look.

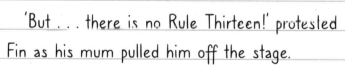

Rule Thirteen states that sore losers are not permitted on the stage so please step away.

'But . . . there is no Rule Thirteen!' protested Fin as his mum pulled him off the stage.

'Nice lie,' said Kabir, attempting and failing to get the mayor to give him a high five.

28. Kebabs and Flying Saucers

Afterwards, Kabir went with Najin to get some celebratory kebabs while I went home with Stink to get rid of Ellis and the troll. We rolled them through the fairy door like two hairy marbles.

Stink looked up at me. 'I guess it's my turn now,' she said, her Silver Bullet wings drooping.

She looked so sad that I found myself saying, 'You can come with me to Professor Najin's if you like, but you've got to promise to go back to Fairyland this evening.'

'YES!' Stink cried zipping round my room then coming back to hover in front of my face. 'I PROMISE, Danny.' Then she grabbed each side of my nose, stared deep into my eyes and said . . .

And you can trust me because fairies NEVER lie.

So that's how I ended up in Najin's garden eating a doner kebab and passing cheesy chips up to Stink who was back in my hair.

When Najin spotted me slipping a chip in there she just shook her head and muttered, 'You're a strange boy, Danny Todd.'

Najin was happy if a bit baffled about winning the race. 'I've encountered a few rogue waves in my time, but never a whopper like that one!' she said. She was so happy that she got chatty and told me and Kabir that she was a professor of marine biology, which was pretty cool, and then she showed us the cups she'd won for sailing. Apparently she was so good she was nearly in the Olympics. In fact, Najin was in such a good mood, she let us drink Dr Pepper out of her trophies, and when Fin and Poppy peered over the garden fence, this is what they saw.

Their eyes flicked around then settled on the foxes who were sunbathing on the lawn. Luckily all of them had turned back to their usual ginger.

'Dad's rung the council again,' said Poppy.

'They're sending pest control round right now,' said Fin.

'TO POISON YOUR FOXES!' they said in unison before disappearing below the fence.

It was a good job they moved so fast because Stink had already stuck her head out from my hair and pulled out her wand. I had the feeling she was about to Green Sixteen them.

And that's when the doorbell rang.

'Is it them?' I said, alarmed. 'Pest control?'

'Probably,' hissed Najin. 'Keep very quiet. They might go away.'

But then we heard Jasper Budgen calling from his house, 'The old lady and her foxes are in the back garden. You can let yourself in round the side.'

The next thing we knew the back gate was being rattled.

Najin leaped to her feet. 'I'll try to stall them!' she said. 'You boys get rid of the foxes!'

Kabir and I ran around the garden, clapping our hands and trying to shoo the foxes out of the back gate, but they refused to budge. They looked at us through sleepy eyes, their tails wagging as if this was some fun game.

Shoo!

'Stink,' I said, shaking her out of my hair. 'You've got to help us!'

Voices were approaching from the side of the house. Najin was arguing with someone. 'I'm telling you there are no foxes in my garden!' she said.

But there were. There were loads of them.

'Leave this to me, Danny!' yelled Stink and she shot out of my hair, threw her wand in an arc and yelled,

'YEEEEEELLLLLLLLLOOOWWWW!!!'

One by one the foxes vanished from sight as they shrank down to the size of frogs. Then Kabir and I dropped to our knees and shoved them in our pockets.

The green smoke faded just as Najin led a woman in a boiler suit into the garden. She was carrying a large bag with MOUSE ARREST PEST CONTROL written on it.

'SEE!' said Najin. 'There are no foxes. I'm afraid Jasper Budgen lives in a fantasy world. He can't be trusted.'

'It's true,' I said, holding tight to the squirming foxes in my pocket. 'Right now he's dressed as Willy Wonka. He thinks he owns a chocolate factory.'

The woman from Mouse Arrest glanced over the fence into the Budgens' garden. Chocolate was everywhere. The fountain was still whirring and pick 'n' mix and Oreos were scattered across the usually immaculate lawn.

Suddenly Jasper Budgen leaped on to his patio. His purple velvet suit and top hat were covered in smears of melted chocolate.

'Have you found them?' he asked, his eyes darting around. 'Her garden's literally crawling in foxes. Yesterday I saw a pink one on the roof of her shed and it was curled up next to a rainbow one.'

'You see,' I whispered to the woman from Mouse Arrest. 'He makes stuff up all the time. It's best to go along with whatever he says.'

Jasper picked up a half-eaten bar of Dairy Milk and began to chomp away on it. 'Sorry about the mess,' he said, waving his hand around.

Apparently a platinum diamond encrusted LEGO man found his way into my chocolate fountain and the Oompa Loompas and I got into a scuffle with a slippery boy.

'See!' I hissed.

The woman nodded. 'Don't worry yourself, Mr Budgen!' she called over the fence. 'I've rounded up all the foxes and put poison down.' She paused here to wink at us. 'They won't be troubling you now.'

'What about the pink one?' he asked.

Yep. Got that one too.

'And the spotty one? This morning I saw the spotty one walking across my lawn, bold as brass.'

'I've definitely got the spotty one,' said the woman.

'About time too!' said Jasper, then he strode
back inside his house, pausing to grab a bag of
chocolate buttons off the patio.

The Mouse Arrest woman
stayed for a trophy of Dr
Pepper then went off to
sort out a nest of mice.

'Where are the foxes?'
asked Najin. 'What did you do
with them? Are they in the shed?'

'Nah,' said Kabir. 'The fairy in Danny's hair
shrank them down and now they're in our
pockets.'

'A fairy shrank them did she?' Najin snorted
and rolled her eyes. 'As long as they're safe,
that's all that matters.'

'They're fine,' I said. 'But we'd better go
before they grow back to their normal size.'

Najin cackled. 'You boys!' she said, giving us
hearty pats on the back. 'If you get a couple
of life jackets you can come round tomorrow

and I'll teach you to use that SUP board. And perhaps we could think about getting the *Hot Rod* out of the river and fixing her. With you two helping me I might be able to do it.'

Then she went inside to watch *Pirates of the Caribbean: Dead Man's Chest*.

As soon as she was gone, Stink flew in front of my face. 'I'd like to help fix the *Hot Rod*, Danny.'

'Well, you can't. You're going back to Fairyland.'

'Oh,' she said sadly. 'Do I have to?'

'Yes,' I said. 'I let you come to the party, didn't I?'

Realising that she had only minutes of freedom left in Humanyworld, Stink made the most of it. First she drank the dregs of Dr Pepper from the trophies. Then she flew into the Budgens' garden and reappeared a few minutes later with a party bag full of pick 'n' mix.

Then
she turned a
seagull blue.

'OK,' she said,
sticking an entire
jazzy in her mouth.
'I'm ready. Let's go.'

I said goodbye to
Kabir outside my house,
but only after he'd handed over all of his tiny
foxes.

'See you tomorrow for our SUP,' he said. 'Now
I've lost my skateboard I might get into supping.
I reckon I'll be amazing at it. I'll probably SUP to
France . . . Or Spain . . . Or Hawaii.'

'Yeah, probably,' I said. There was no point
arguing with The Kid when he was on a roll.

And then I raced up to my bedroom. I had a
plan, but if it was going to work I needed to act
fast.

29.
Lots of Horses

'I suppose I have to go,' said Stink, eyeing the fairy door. She was sitting on my bed sharing the last of her sweets with Sophie.

'NOOOOOO!' cried Sophie.

'Danny's making me,' said Stink, her eyes all big and sad.

'Danny's a horrid poo head!' said Sophie.

Stink gave this some thought, then said. 'No, he's not really. You're lucky he's your brother, Soph. Fandango is the horrid poo head.'

Then Stink emptied
the sherbert from a flying
saucer into her mouth
and flew up in front of my
face. 'Thanks, Danny,' she said.
'It's been a laugh. I like it here in Humanyland.
You're nice to me.'

For a second I considered letting Stink stay,
but I could see my blazer hanging on the back
of my chair, ready for school on Monday, and
my unicorn rucksack peeping out of my cupboard.

It was sad, but there really was no place for a
fairy in my life.

And, if I'm being completely honest, it hadn't
been a laugh. Mainly it had been massively
stressful.

Plus, of course, my
pockets were still full
of foxes.

'It's been interesting
meeting you,' I said,

and I stuck out my finger so that Stink could
shake it between her two little hands.

Then she fluttered down to the floor and
opened the door. The Fairyland funk drifted out.
'Bye, Danny,' she said. 'Bye, Soph.'

'Wait. I've got a present for you,' I said, then
I took the foxes out of my pocket and put them
carefully on the floor.

Stink gasped and Sophie squealed.

'Are all those horses for me?' asked Stink.
'Fandango will be blue with envy when he sees
me with them. I can ride a different one every
day! I'll train them. I'll be their chief. I won't be

S dot Tink the bad fairy. I'll be S dot Tink the horse fairy!'

The tiny foxes didn't need any encouragement. Drawn by the pong of Fairy Land they galloped through the door without a backward glance.

Then, after, gazing at me, Sophie and Humanyworld for one last time, Stink said, 'Bye, Danny Todd, best of humans and his funny sister!' Then she walked through the fairy door and it slammed shut behind her.

All evening I've been patting my hair, just to check there are no fairies in there.

There aren't. Stink's gone.

So now it's just me, Noah and Tony up in my

bedroom. I start secondary school the day after tomorrow and I reckon I'll be all right. After all, I released a fairy from Fairyland, and a troll and a gnome, and then I got them all to go back again. Plus let's not forget the foxes I removed humanely from Najin's garden.

I've got skills.

Goodnight, Diary, and goodbye.

My strange times are over!

30.
Monday

My strange times aren't over.
Today was my first ever day
at secondary school.

To begin with things went
well. Kabir and I found out
we were in the same form
group and no one laughed
at my rucksack. A big Year
Eleven boy did say, 'Nice shoes,
dingleweed!' but it could have
been a compliment.

But a surprising thing happened
at lunchtime.

Kabir and I were sitting in the packed canteen
getting ready to eat our lunch.

'Mum made me a Milky Bar sandwich,' said

Kabir, unwrapping clingfilm.

'Are you sure?' I said, 'because it looks like cheese.'

Kabir scoffed. 'You want your eyes testing, mate!'

I looked down and opened my own lunch box wondering if Dad had put a boiled egg in there.

'Hello, Danny Todd!'

Relaxing on a bed of Frubes and Cheestrings was Stink.

I slammed my lunch box shut, then opened the lid again.

She was still there. And this time I noticed she'd made shoes out of grapes and a pastrami cloak.

'What are you doing?' I whispered. 'You promised that once you'd earned one hundred nuggets you'd go away for good.'

'Yeah? Well I LIED, Danny!' she said with a grin. 'One thing you should know about fairies is that we never tell the truth. You're my boy, and you're NEVER *EVER* getting rid of me!'

Which is just great.

LOOK OUT FOR
STINK 2

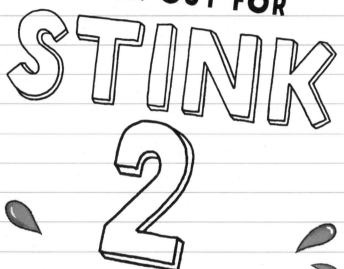

COMING SOON . . .

Mystic Ginger is a cloak-wearing fox who always ends up in big trouble. I've made 135 Mystic Ginger comics and here are a few of them.

You should draw some cartoons of your own. It's fun because you can make ANYTHING happen!

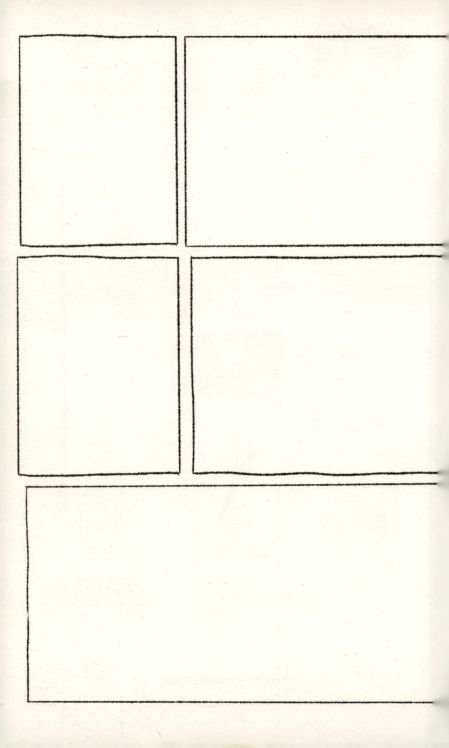

Acknowledgements

Writers hate repeating words because it sounds bad. Unfortunately, I've had so much help with Stink that I am going to have to use the word 'thank you' a lot. To get round this, I'm going to replace each 'thank you' with a piece of fruit.

When I told my agent, Julia Churchill, that I wanted to write a book 'and draw the pictures' she didn't laugh heartily, but instead shared the idea with Liz Bankes and Lindsey Heaven. These three fantastic women have made my childhood dream come true. Strawberry!

Kiwi to my brilliant editors, Liz Bankes and Sarah Levison; you helped me take Stink to some wild places. I would also like to give a huge pineapple to Stink's wonderful graphic designer, Ryan Hammond, who not only made Stink look awesome, but who kindly and oh-so-patiently guided me through the process of illustrating a book.

Cherry to the team at Farshore who share my love of stories, laughter and troll poo jokes: Olivia Carson, Pippa Poole, Rory Codd, Aleena Hasan, Olivia Adams, Lucy Courtenay, Hannah Penny – a big stinky kiss to you all!

I would like to banana my seaside crew: Helen Barker for the walks and Helen Dennis for the talks, Abie Longstaff for her wise advice, and my mum and dad for picking up my children from school and me from the station. You are all a huge support to me.

Kumquat to my inspiring nephews and nieces: Eric, Audrey, Mara, Rowan and the real Danny and Sophie. The funny things you do and say give me lots of ideas. I hope you like the picture of Danny on the waterslide. I drew it for you as a way of saying grapefruit.

My biggest raspberry goes to Ben, Nell and Flora. If Stink is full of fun, joy and silly jokes, it is because I share my life with you. Aren't I lucky?

Don't miss . . .

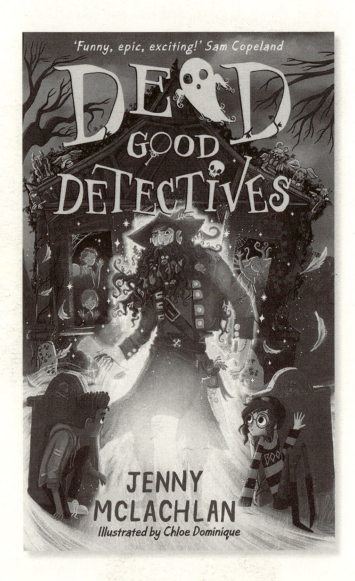

'Funny, epic, exciting!' Sam Copeland

DEAD
GOOD
DETECTIVES

JENNY
MCLACHLAN

Illustrated by Chloe Dominique

Join the adventure . . .

JENNY MCLACHLAN

is the author of the bestselling Roar series and
Dead Good Detectives, as well as several acclaimed
teen novels. Stink is her first author-illustrated novel.
Before Jenny became a writer she was an English
teacher; she now lives by the seaside and enjoys
writing, drawing pictures, and day-dreaming on the
South Downs with her dog, Maggie.